Shan Dara

Tenba

D0559983

Jett

Orie

Buddy

THE CAT MASTER

THE CAT MASTER

by Bonnie Pemberton

Marshall Cavendish

Text copyright © 2007 by Bonnie Pemberton • All rights reserved. No part of this book may be reproduced or transmitted in any form or by any means, electronic or mechanical, including photocopying, recording, or by any information storage and retrieval system, without permission in writing from the publisher.
• Marshall Cavendish Corporation • 99 White Plains Road • Tarrytown, NY 10591 • www.marshallcavendish.us • This book is a work of fiction. Names, characters, places, and incidents are products of the author's imagination and are used fictitiously. Any resemblance to actual events or locales or persons, living or dead, is entirely coincidental. • Library of Congress Cataloging-in-Publication Data • Pemberton, Bonnie. • The Cat Master / by Bonnie Pemberton. — 1st ed. • p. cm. • Summary: Buddy and Jett, two cat brothers (one evil, one good), vie for the title of Cat Master as a retinue of dogs, cats, a possum, a bird, and a lizard help restore a monarch to his rightful throne. • ISBN-13: 978-0-7614-5340-6 • [1. Cats— Fiction. 2. Brothers—Fiction. 3. Animals—Fiction. 4. Fantasy.] I. Title. • PZ7.P36147Cat 2007 [Fic]—dc22 • 2006026562 • The text of this book is set in Garamond. • Book design by Sonia Chaghatzbanian • Endpaper artwork by Lisa Falkenstern • Printed in China • First edition • 10 9 8 7 6 5 4 3 2

mc Marshall Cavendish

*To my parents, Olive and Clyde Pemberton
and my aunt, Janice Holmes*

In memory of Buddy

ACKNOWLEDGMENTS

THE DEPICTION OF ANIMAL CONTROL OFFICERS IN THIS BOOK IS FICTIONAL, AND IN NO WAY REFLECTS THE TRUE NATURE OF THESE DEDICATED PROFESSIONALS OR THEIR COMMITMENT TO ANIMAL WELFARE.

THERE ARE MANY PEOPLE who helped bring *The Cat Master* to life, and though I can't mention them all by name, they know who they are, and I will always be grateful. Special thanks go to: my agent, the indomitable Anne Hawkins, who took an unknown author with a story about cats and never stopped fighting until it was published; my brilliant editor, Margery Cuyler, for her respect, unblinking vision, and meticulous professionalism; my dear friend and fellow author, Sharon Rowe, whose love, loyalty, and wisdom have never failed me; my pals at Trinity Writers' Workshop, whose invaluable critiques and unfailing enthusiasm helped make *The Cat Master*'s publication a reality; Tom and Peggy Laskoski, whose home is a sanctuary of camaraderie and support; my cousin, Niki Kantzios, and our shared childhood of animals, books, and imagination; my husband, Kipp Baker; daughter, Kristin; son-in-law, Mark; and all the Baker/Pemberton clan whose love, laughter, and acceptance have made my heart so full. And finally, to Buddy, the stray cat who changed my life forever.

THE CAT MASTER

PROLOGUE

THE OLD CAT STAGGERED through the alley, a bright Texas moon lighting his way. His coat, once a lustrous black and white, was now matted with burrs, and his eyes, once a startling blue, were opaque with age. Twenty years had passed since he had been chosen as Cat Master, and his reign was coming to an end. Disoriented, he paused, head up, his nose probing the air. The scent of roses blew his way, and he sighed with gratitude. As always, Mother Wind was with him, and blindly the cat followed her lead to the sheltering tangle of blooms. Hiding beneath their thorny canes, he panted with fatigue.

As spiritual leader of his species, he had given thousands of felines hope and courage in their times of need. And now, in these last moments, he hoped he could do the same for himself. The old cat smiled, remembering how surprised he'd been at his coronation so many years ago. As a simple Feral, he'd been frightened by his anointed role as the great leader and unsure if he was truly qualified to serve. But the natural world had hummed with animal telepathy, and Mother

Wind, who watched over all creatures, had led his mind through the noise, teaching him to decipher only felines' cries for help and insight.

A soft breeze ruffled his fur, and a sprinkle of petals fell from the bush. "Thank you, Mother," he whispered. Wincing with pain he eased down onto their welcome softness.

The old cat drew a ragged breath. How many times had his mind-talk comforted the sick and dying and spoken to their hearts of Sho-valla, the holy resting place of all animals? Now it was his turn to go, and he was strangely troubled. Not by death—he had no fear of that—but he'd worked hard to keep order and peace among his species, and there was much left undone.

Hostility had grown between the Feral and the Indoor, and though the old Cat Master had failed to quell the anger that simmered between them, there was one last thing he intended to try—something that could happen only after his death. He groaned, shifting to a more comfortable position. At least his lineage had produced a worthy successor. He thought of the last litter he'd sired only three years before. Two of the males impressed him. Both were strong, fearless, and intelligent, but only one had shown compassion and humility as well.

A vicelike pressure gripped his chest. It was time. Fighting to stand, he pushed his mind through the darkness, until soft and probing, he found his young successor's soul. *Rise from the alley, my son,* he called. *Of all my blood, you are The Chosen!* At first, he felt only the tenderness of connection, but suddenly, another mind slithered between him and his heir; one so evil and full of rage that it wrenched them apart. Something was wrong! The old cat tried to reconnect, to send a warning, but a searing pain squeezed his heart, and he fell to his side. His heir was in danger and needed to be told, but already the old tom's soul was slipping toward Sho-valla.

"Your reign begins, my son," he gasped. "May Mother help you through the darkness to come."

ONE

BUDDY JOLTED FROM SLEEP, heart pounding, ears forward and alert.

A breeze rustled through the magnolia tree, and a dying loop of ivy flopped listlessly against the glass panes, but otherwise the early August morning was quiet. No monster lumbered through the neighborhood; there was nothing to explain the lingering dread now tightening the muscles of his neck.

"Everything's fine," the yellow cat whispered with false bravado. "It was just a dream." Arching his back, he stretched. "Snap out of it; shake it off, calm down." His pulse still pounded, and he considered finding his catnip-stuffed mouse. A quick snort of that always relaxed him.

Beside him, The Boy lay snoring, unaware of murky dreams or whispering voices, and Buddy squinted against the shaft of sunlight bathing them both in a blast of Texas summer.

Despite the cat's best efforts to relax, his skin twitched with anxiety. "Get ahold of yourself, Buddy." He kneaded The Boy's pillow for comfort. "Just a nightmare, everyone has those occasionally." Only the dream hadn't really been bad . . . or had it?

Rise from the alley . . .

Wispy fragments of a loving voice resonated in his mind. Things had started out fine, then something strange had happened, something unsettling. But what?

Licking his chops, Buddy focused on The Boy's cheerful room. Sci-fi posters covered bright yellow walls, plaid curtains snapped and fluttered against the windowsill, and tangles of jeans, T-shirts, and socks overflowed an open drawer. A typical morning. Everything in order. Jumping lightly to the floor, the polished wood felt cool on Buddy's paws as he trotted to the hallway. "Just a dream," he reminded himself, which was true. "Nothing unusual," he added . . . which, of course, he knew was a lie.

It was almost morning, and Zekki and Pris scrambled through the living room, jumping onto furniture, skidding across end tables, and vaulting onto curtains.

"Got you!" Pris squealed, grabbing Zekki's luxurious tail and crashing into a potted plant.

The cats rolled on the carpet, eyes wild, hind legs kicking, as tufts of fur coated the furniture in a subtle haze of white and brown. With grunts and growls they thrashed in circles, finally toppling the plant, which fell forward, spraying the carpet with fine, moist dirt. Eyes wild, both animals scattered in surprise.

"That was good," the little female calico said, creeping from beneath a chair. "I really got you that time."

"I let you." Zekki eyed the couch. "Do you think they're up yet?"

Creeping to the doorway, Pris peeked around the corner. "I don't see anyone, but hurry up."

"I'll do my best." Claws out, Zekki stretched his white body against the sofa, hooking the creamy linen fabric and enjoying his slow, steady picking of the material. The rhythmic clutch-and-pull was so hypnotic he almost didn't hear the voice from the shadows.

"Do you want to be declawed?"

Zekki froze with guilt before sprinting away. "I was just—"

"I know what you were doing." Buddy stood silhouetted in the doorway, face stern and set. "But don't do it again." Quickly, he rubbed against the sofa's tattered material, trying to smooth down the wayward threads and nudge fragments of gauzy stuffing back into place.

The white cat turned in frustration. "I don't care if I get declawed. I'm an Indoor, remember? We don't get to do any- thing, anyway."

Buddy sighed. All indoor cats went through a period of longing for the outdoors, or Outs, as they called it, but usually it passed. For Zekki it hadn't, and he spent an increasing amount of time staring through windows, his eyes dark with discontent.

"We don't choose our destiny," Buddy said softly. "All animals have instinctual knowledge of humans and their world, but Indoors are much more informed than Ferals. We have television, radio, food, protection—"

"I know all that," Zekki cut in. "And I don't want to be ungrateful or anything, but what good's information if you can never use it?" He turned toward the yellow tom, eyes worshipful. "You've been in the Outs, you had lots of adventures before The Boy found you. Tell us about the alley and . . ."

Rise from the alley . . .

Tangled memories of both the Outs and the dream floated behind Buddy's eyes, and he suddenly felt irritable and tired. "That was a long time ago, Zekki. I don't mind sharing an occasional story, but I don't want to talk about it today."

"Why not?" Zekki's tone was challenging.

A bedroom door slammed, and all three cats jumped, poised to bolt.

"It's just The Boy," Pris whispered. She gave Zekki a gentle nudge. "We don't need a story today, do we? We'll talk about something else, okay?"

Zekki gave a sullen shrug, and Buddy's tail swished the floor with agitation.

"Now everybody's mad!" the calico wailed, looking from one cat to the other. "Are you mad?"

Buddy sighed, his annoyance giving way to guilt. The young cats rarely pushed him about anything; he was being unfair. He made a mental note to tell them a good story soon, maybe something about hunting. "I'm not mad, Pris, just hungry. Let's have breakfast and then meet in the den for our morning lessons."

"Can we talk about The Cat Master?" Zekki's voice was

still bold. "I've decided if I ever get out, I'm going to find him."

A nerve twitched beneath Buddy's eye, and a muddy recollection flared, then sputtered and died. "No one 'finds' The Cat Master, Zekki. He speaks to us through our minds. Eventually you'll learn telepathic talk, but today we're discussing The Wind."

"Again?" The white cat rolled his eyes. "For gosh sakes, we're always talking about—" His words were stopped by a well-aimed slap to his ear, and he yowled in surprise.

Buddy leaned forward, one sinewy paw still poised to strike. "Never speak with disrespect for The Wind!" He turned to include Pris, cowed beneath a chair. "She's the breath that guides us, and no animal can live in the world without Her."

Laughter floated from the kitchen. Plates clattered, cabinets banged, and the rich fragrance of bacon filled the hallway.

The cats crouched in awkward silence.

"I'm sorry," Zekki finally mumbled. "I don't know why I said that."

Anger fading, Buddy stepped back. "It's hot, and we're all a little stressed today. Go on and eat."

Usually, nothing squelched the young cats' enthusiasm for food, but today they skulked toward the kitchen, tails dragging, shoulders hunched. Buddy watched them go, his heart heavy with remorse. How had the morning started out so wrong? Jumping on the couch, he settled himself against a bright coral pillow. And why was he so uncomfortable with

Zekki's questions? The alley, though dangerous, was only a place, and The Cat Master was a powerful spiritual figure that all cats should understand. Splaying a hind foot, Buddy carefully licked between each toe, methodically moving up the leg and onto his flank. It was every adult feline's duty to teach the young about all aspects of feline life. Hadn't his mother said that an ill-informed cat would soon be a dead one? He stopped grooming, suddenly confused. Was it his mother who said that, or had it been his mate, Ahn-ya?

Rise from the alley . . .

Tension tightened his shoulders, and he nuzzled beneath a cushion. Why was he thinking about the alley, anyway? He was an indoor cat.

You're a Feral . . . Unwanted thoughts hissed in his head . . .

"I'm an Indoor!" he said loudly, voice firm and slightly strident.

The Boy stuck his head around the corner. "Is that you, Bud?" He looked concerned. "Are you hungry? You wanna eat?"

Jumping to the floor, Buddy rubbed against The Boy's ankles until pale, thin arms scooped him into a hug.

"I am an Indoor," he thought fiercely, burying his head in the child's soft white T-shirt . . . and this time his troubled thoughts were silent.

TWO

JETT CROUCHED BENEATH the magnolia tree, his dark form barely outlined by the moon. It had taken months, but the big, gray tom had finally detected Buddy's scent wafting from the Sixth Avenue house. Carefully, he tested the wind. If he wasn't careful, Buddy would be able to identify the gray cat by his scent. That was the annoying thing about Mother, he thought, making sure he was downwind of the house. She never took sides. Satisfied with his position, Jett settled into the grass, his mind whirring.

It had finally happened. The old Cat Master was dead, and a successor had been chosen. Jett knew this was true, because after countless tries, he'd managed to tap into the old Master's mind-talk as he was dying. Even now, his pulse raced with excitement at what he'd heard. The ancient leader had made a serious blunder. The Law plainly said that only a Feral could be named as Cat Master, and Buddy was definitely no longer feral. Jett considered something else that could work in his favor. His mental intrusion had caused a telepathic blip in the old Master's announcement. It was possible that Buddy still didn't realize he'd been chosen. Indoors often had trouble deciphering mind-talk. Sometimes they didn't hear things the Ferals had known for years. Either way, both glitches worked to Jett's advantage. In three days the Cat Master's coronation would take place at The Gathering. If Buddy didn't appear, Jett would automatically ascend as the last surviving male in the old Master's final litter. A firefly winked in the darkness, and Jett snapped it from the air with one bite, munching the insect with pleasure. Though this scenario was preferable, there could still be trouble if Buddy ever learned the truth. There was nothing in The Law prohibiting him from returning to the Outs at any time to claim his rightful title. Jett licked the last flecks of the firefly off his paw and smiled. But Buddy *would* be at The Gathering. Jett would make sure that he was, and, this time, his plan for Buddy's defeat would happen without the unpredictability of battle. He frowned, remembering his last attempt on Buddy's life and how badly the attack had failed. Not only had the yellow tom escaped, but Jett had been badly wounded. Painful memories slid through his mind.

Months had passed since his injury, and though his wounds had healed, the trauma was raw and deep. Usually his days were spent in depressed indifference, but a broken mirror lay in the alley and Jett watched from a distance, drawn to its glinting surface. He had seen his reflection before, but only in water. Curious, he crept to the glass . . . and looked down. A ghoulish parody of his once-regal face stared back. From the left side of his nose a brooding eye burned with misery. The right eye was gone, replaced by an empty socket that sank like an oozing crater beneath his brow. Horrified, Jett ran from the alley, scaling fences and dodg-

ing cars before diving beneath an overturned box in a shed. For many days he hid within its bleak obscurity; silent, bitter, and afraid. When he finally emerged, a murky peace had filled his soul . . . and with it some valuable information: Death was nothing when compared to humiliation, and there were many kinds of scars. His time in isolation had produced a brand-new plan: Jett would bide his time, take all that Buddy held dear, and then condemn him to . . . live.

The big cat sighed with satisfaction. Patience had prevailed. The old Master was finally dead, and Buddy had made a fatal mistake; he had dared to step indoors. Jett would simply lure him to The Gathering and expose him for the cowardly imposter he was. No Feral in his right mind would allow an Indoor to rule, no matter what the old Master had said. The Law was The Law! Prickles of pleasure surged through the gray tom's body. He stretched in the soft grass, envisioning himself as the omnipotent ruler. He would be powerful, adored, and respected, while Buddy would slink into the shadows, disgraced, alone, and reviled by his kind.

From inside the house, Buddy jumped onto the windowsill and stared toward the magnolia.

Jett shrank back. He wasn't ready to be seen. Not quite yet. Slinking closer to the house, he slithered between two bushes and under the porch, until he lay beneath the casement where the yellow cat now sat. A glowing light shone from the bedroom, illuminating Buddy's shiny coat and well-fed form. This was in sharp contrast to Jett's matted fur and protruding ribs. His pulse quickened with hatred. The sooner Buddy was gone, the better, but drawing him into the Outs was going to be difficult.

Movement behind the curtains caught his attention, and Jett sank into the shadows. A white cat and a calico joined Buddy on the windowsill, their demeanor relaxed and friendly. They were obviously adolescents, and they jostled for position as the yellow cat lovingly groomed them.

The big tom stifled a laugh. An idea had suddenly taken form.

The house was quiet in the steamy darkness. Mrs. O'Connell had turned out the lights long ago, and The Boy lay sleeping on his back, a thin sheen of sweat on his upper lip.

Normally, Buddy would have curled up beside him, their breathing rhythmic and calm, but the morning's dream still haunted the tom, leaving him confused, frightened, and unable to sleep. Feeling the suffocating presence long before seeing it, Buddy watched from The Boy's bedroom window . . . and realized with a sense of detachment that the dream was only the beginning.

In the den a clock chimed one, and as if on cue, the thing beneath the tree moved. Pressing hard against the screen, Buddy tensed, ears flat to his skull, pupils dilated, searching.

The sinewy figure glided behind the trunk, circled a holly and appeared in a snarl of shadows by the house. "Come out, come out, wherever you are," a smoky voice purred from the darkness. "You didn't think you could hide forever, did you?"

That voice! Buddy leaned against the wall, his heart hammering. Long repressed memories thrashed their way to the surface. "I'm asleep," he whispered to himself, knowing full well he wasn't.

From the bed, The Boy mumbled incoherently, kicking

rumpled covers to the floor and flopping with a grunt onto his belly.

Buddy waited until the child was settled, then turned toward the window, his tongue parched with dread. "What are you doing here, Jett?"

"Not a very hospitable greeting." The tone was pleasant, but malice pulsed beneath its smooth veneer. "I thought you'd be glad to see someone from the old neighborhood, because once Mother brought me your scent, I couldn't wait to see *you*." Leaves crackled, and the form disappeared behind a stand of ferns.

Buddy vaulted across The Boy's legs and onto another sill for a clearer view.

"And what a sight it is." A gleaming eye blinked from the greenery. "Our esteemed Buddy, the pick of the litter, is now an *Indoor*. I'll bet you even have your own shiny food bowl and lots of little toys." The voice dripped with contempt. "I can smell the stink of human from here."

Buddy stiffened. "I didn't have much choice, if you remember."

Jett sighed. "Yes, that was an unfortunate incident. Of course, Ahn-ya was devastated by your sudden disappearance, as we all were, but you'll be pleased to know that she turned to me for comfort and forgot about you very soon. Too bad you can't see her," he crooned. "She's matured into such a beautiful cat." His voice thickened with innuendo. "Her devotion to me is almost embarrassing."

Outrage constricted Buddy's throat. Gentle Ahn-ya, so defenseless and alone.

"As a matter of fact," Jett's voice continued, "I find I've developed a real taste for things you love." Sudden laughter cut the stillness. "Like your little friends, for instance. You're very fond of them, aren't you?"

There was menace in the question, and Buddy's mind raced to decipher its meaning.

"I've noticed the white one looks out the windows a lot."

"Leave them alone!" Buddy pushed his head against the screen, his eyes straining against the darkness.

"But they're so attractive, especially the calico." The direction of the sound changed in midsentence and floated from the right of the casement. "I don't know if I can help myself."

"I'm warning you . . ."

"You're warning *me?*" Jett's voice was mockingly incredulous. "No, no," he whispered, rising slowly on powerful haunches and glaring through the screen. "I'm warning *you*." A massive paw touched the brick for balance. "I'll come back, you pathetic imposter. And when I do, things you love will suffer!" With a shriek of fury, Jett sprang toward the screen, his claws grazing the wire, then landed heavily in the bushes.

Startled from sleep, The Boy reached for the lamp, which crashed to the floor in a shatter of ceramic. "Buddy?" Flailing hands groped in the darkness. "Bud! Come here, boy. What's going on?"

Dodging his grasp, Buddy dashed into the hall where Zekki and Pris crouched against the wall, fur rumpled from sleep.

"What is it, what's happening?" Pris peeped.

"Stay away from the windows!" Careening into the dining room, Buddy leaped to a sideboard and moved the curtain aside with his nose.

The yard stretched serenely beneath the moonlight. Stars

winked in the velvet sky, and a gentle wind caressed the magnolia. No movement. Nothing unusual.

"What's wrong with the windows?" Zekki asked, frozen with fear. "I don't understand."

"Just do what I tell you!" Jumping down, the yellow tom sprinted from room to room, peering through screens, sniffing beneath doors.

Lights went on and footsteps scuffled from the bedrooms.

"Mom, something's wrong!" The Boy called.

Darting under a credenza, Buddy hunkered beneath its protection. He'd thought he was safe with The Boy, but it was all starting again. Why? What had brought this malevolence back into his life? Beside him the catnip mouse lay shrouded in dust, one plastic eye staring out in silence. Suddenly ashamed, he pushed it away.

Rise from the alley . . .

Buddy's pulse quickened.

The dream; something about the alley. He tried to capture the memory, but the words fluttered like moths into nothingness.

Floorboards creaked, and Mrs. O'Connell's fuzzy blue house shoes shuffled past. "Buddy's here somewhere, honey; we'll find him in the morning. Go back to sleep."

Doors slammed, and the house was quiet once more. Or was it?

A trash can clattered in the alley.

Something snickered from the porch.

In the distance Buddy heard Zekki and Pris running through the house, their frantic activity driven by uncertainty. He would have to tell them something, he thought, crawling into the open and scurrying toward the kitchen, but for the moment he didn't know what.

Jumping to the sink, Buddy stared through the slatted blinds.

Evil had come to Sixth Avenue, familiar as his heartbeat . . . alien as the moon.

The crawl space beneath the kitchen was unusually hot and
stuffy. Muffled noises seeped through the vents, disrupting
the quiet, and the lizard twisted inside a moldy workman's
cap trying to get back to sleep. Above him the thumping
continued. The Boy and his mother were bad enough, he
thought, squinting with fury—always lurching around on
big white feet, slamming doors, and banging pots and pans.
He'd watched them for a long time, and even though they
hadn't died, which was his continuing prayer, they had at
least kept normal hours.

But not the cats.

He stared with unmasked hatred at the ceiling of the
crawl space, listening to the rapid footsteps rippling above.
They were at it day and night. "Let's scratch the furniture!
Let's play with the plants!"

"I know something fun," he snorted, twisting onto his
side and pounding a wad of insulation into a pillow. "Let's
play Kitty-in-the-Fireplace." This was a game he played
often, with endless variety. He yawned and stretched. There
was Kitty-in-the-Ice-Storm, Kitty-in-the-Toilet, and then, of
course, his all-time favorite: Kitty-in-the-Dentist-Chair.
"Pests," he muttered, closing his eyes. "Jumping around,
knocking things over." By the time he got to Kitty-in-the-
Disposal, he was fast asleep, his squeaky snores spraying tiny
puffs of dust into the tepid air.

T H R E E

SOMETHING WAS WRONG WITH BUDDY, and The Boy was worried. "Hey!" he called, "Bud didn't eat his food again!"

"Leave him alone!" his mother shouted from the bedroom. "He'll eat when he gets hungry!"

"Yeah, well he didn't sleep with me again last night, either," he muttered. Maybe his mom was right; maybe it would all blow over like last time. He frowned at the unhappy memory. Traumatized, is what the vet had said when The Boy had first found Buddy. Dehydrated, in shock, maybe even brain damaged—and he seemed a lot like that now, running around, looking desperate, not eating. But eventually, he reminded himself, Buddy had settled down, learned to play, even bonded with Pris and Zekki. "I know he's been happy here," The Boy said out loud. But was it true?

Shuffling to the den, he flopped into a recliner. The dark green leather felt cool against his bare thighs, and placing both hands on the chair's plush arms, he pushed back until his body was almost flat. Closing his eyes, he crossed his long, thin legs at the ankles. Dad used to watch television here, he thought. The recollection was painful, because when The Boy was only ten, his father had run off with some woman, and no one had seen him since. But right about then he'd found Buddy, and after that, things hadn't hurt so bad. Picking at a scab, he considered the last two years. He'd never had a friend like Bud, ever, and though he was careful not to mention it to his pals, he knew Buddy was more than a pet, much more. That was clear from the very beginning. Even his mom said they could read each other's minds. Twisting his head, The Boy eyed the cat crouched in a golden lump by the glass patio door. "What's wrong, Bud?" he said quietly.

One yellow ear flicked, but that was all.

The Boy's thoughts poked and pushed for answers, but it was no use. Buddy's mind was closed; a locked drawer with only the tip of something showing, something the child had never seen but vaguely understood. Pushing his chair to an upright position, he tried again. "Here, boy." He patted his stomach. "Don't you want to come up here with me?"

Buddy didn't respond, but Pris and Zekki galloped from the hallway, jumped on his lap, and jostled for position. They seemed desperate for attention, and he rubbed their ears. His mom had said everything would be okay, so why was he feeling so weird? A dull memory wormed through his mind, and he sat up so quickly that the young cats tumbled to the ground. The feeling was the same as when his dad had left! Suddenly panicked, The Boy looked around. Buddy was gone, and even though sunlight still spilled through the glass doors, the place where he'd been seemed cold and dark.

On the third night, Buddy double-checked each room and wandered into the hallway. Above him, a photograph stood on the desk. It was taken shortly after The Boy had found him, and the gaunt feline face staring from the frame was a far cry from the well-fed vision now greeting him from every mirror. How long had he been here? A year? Two? It didn't matter; the young cats' lives were in jeopardy, and there was much to do. He trotted to the den where they both slept curled together on an ottoman. "Wake up. I need to talk to you."

They struggled to their feet, eyes frightened.

"I want you to promise me something."

Pris swallowed. "Promise you what?"

"It's about The Boy. The Boy . . ." He stopped, fighting an unexpected quaver in his voice.

"What about him?" Zekki's tail flicked uneasily.

"The Boy's a very special human. He's gentle and kind and . . . he saved my life. If anything should happen to me, promise you'll be there for The Boy. He counts on us . . ." He paused. "For a lot of things."

The house creaked and shifted, and a clock ticked like a metronome from the den.

"But what could happen to you?" Pris said.

Buddy regarded her earnest face. "Do you remember what I told you about Sho-valla?"

The young cats fidgeted, looking at one another for help.

"It's where all animals go when they die?" Zekki volunteered.

"And what else?"

"No animal is turned away . . ." Pris trailed off.

"And The Cat Master will help us in our journey there," Zekki finished.

Buddy was relieved; they hadn't forgotten. "Sho-valla is holy and not to be used in your games, right?"

"We don't," Pris said quickly. "We never do that."

"And why not?"

"Because it's The Law!" they both yowled with enthusiasm.

"And what is The Law?"

Zekki scrunched his brow. "Sacred rules that all cats live by."

"Yes," Buddy said, "but never do anything just because it's The Law; do it only if you see the *truth* behind The Law. Do you understand?"

Zekki frowned. "I—I think so."

"What about The Wind?" Buddy continued.

"She's our Mother!" the young cats proudly recited in unison. "She warns us of danger, leads us to food, finds our mates, tells us what to run to, and what to run from."

Buddy moved closer. "And how does She do this?"

"Scent and sound!" Pris crowed.

"Listen carefully." Buddy's eyes locked with theirs. "If you're ever in trouble, watch for Her, count on Her. She'll never let you down."

Zekki and Pris stared, pupils huge and shining.

"One more thing." He lowered his voice, and the cats leaned in to hear him. "Sho-valla is the source of the world and all its goodness, and goodness demands respect. However"—he took a breath, eyes unblinking—"there's also

evil in the world, and sometimes it masquerades as right-
eousness pretending to be good. Watch for it, fight it, and
never accept it. Do you understand?"

They nodded.

"You're fine cats," Buddy said. "I'm proud of you both."

"He hasn't really eaten or acted like himself in five days." The
voice leaked through the vents in the crawl space. "I think
we'd better take him to the vet's."

Hunting termites beneath a crossbeam, the lizard
snapped to attention. Had she said "vet"? Scurrying closer,
he stuck his snout through the grate.

"He isn't sick, is he?" a worried voice asked. "He won't
die or anything?"

"Honey, it'll be fine; just get the carrier."

The carrier! They were getting the carrier! Leaping from
the vent, the lizard danced in the dust. They were taking a
cat to the veterinarian, a place where many went and few
returned!

"I can't find it, where is it?" The Boy shouted from
above.

"It's in the garage, you idiots!" the lizard screamed,
pounding the wall.

"Wait a minute." Footsteps clicked toward the door. "It's
in the garage."

"Yes!" he howled, rolling on his back and kicking his legs
with reptilian joy. "They are going!" Above him, there was a
scuffling and the scraping of a chair.

Humming a tune, the lizard planned his day: First, a
little sun . . .

A door slammed, followed by unintelligible conversation.

Then he'd check out the sow bug supply under the roses . . .

An engine rumbled in the driveway.

Maybe he'd even spend some time on the front porch.

Tires crunched on gravel.

The lizard tilted his head, listening to the silence. "One down and two to go!" he shouted, pounding the ground until sunbeams whirled in the dust. A shaft of light shone through a broken windowpane, and he flopped in its narrow warmth. Closing his eyes, he pictured long, peaceful nights with nothing but the sound of crickets to keep him company. It was tragic, he fantasized, but consumed with grief, the remaining cats would probably wither and die. The lizard sat up. Maybe the child and his mother would, too. Claws clasped to his chest, he sighed with pleasure.

Hope was a wonderful thing.

F O U R

THE TWO YOUNG CATS stood motionless in the living room, eyes wide with disbelief.

"Buddy's coming back, right?" Pris squeaked, her round face wrinkled with fear.

Zekki licked his chops. "Sure," he said, trying to sound confident. "They're just taking him to the veterinarian for a . . . a checkup or something. We've been to the vet's before; it wasn't so bad." But he, too, felt a sharp pang of separation. He couldn't remember ever having been without the yellow tom. As adopted kittens their first memory had been of Buddy's gentle face pressed against their carrier, his sleek yellow coat shaded with caramel stripes, his golden eyes radiating friendship and security. Felines rarely knew their fathers, but that's what Buddy had seemed like, and the two young cats had grown to love him. Suddenly the house and its comforting routine seemed strange, and Zekki felt an inexplicable sense of loss.

"It's okay, Pris." He licked the calico's ear. "Buddy wouldn't leave us. The Boy would never let that happen."

The curtains were drawn against the mounting summer heat, and the dark room felt odd amid the bright summer sounds of squealing children and ice-cream carts tinkling through the neighborhood.

For a long moment the two cats sat shoulder to shoulder, their ears scanning for sounds.

"I wish we could at least look out the window," Pris finally said. "But we're not—"

"Wait a minute, wait a minute!" Zekki jumped to his feet, nose quivering. "Look at that!"

In her haste, Mrs. O'Connell had left the front door ajar, forgetting to close the screen door as well. A gentle breeze now blew it open and shut, with only wire between the cats and the porch.

Forgetting their anxiety, Zekki and Pris moved toward the welcome brightness.

Leaves fluttered in the breeze, a branch creaked, and the fragrance of honeysuckle filled the room.

"Having fun?" Gently the question floated in the warm, sweet air.

Pris jumped sideways, skittering behind the sofa. Zekki bristled, poised to run. "Who's there?"

"Come a little closer and see." It was a pleasant enough voice, even friendly, but there was an edgy undercurrent that made Zekki uneasy. He moved toward the sound.

"Don't do it!" Pris wailed. "Buddy said not to go near the windows!"

A condescending chuckle rippled the stillness. "It isn't a window, it's a door, and besides, I'm harmless. There's nothing to be afraid of."

Tail twitching, Zekki inched forward. "Where are you?"

The porch swing swayed in the hot summer breeze, and a cardinal trilled to his mate from a rooftop.

Pris shrank against the couch. "Zek—Zek—Zekki," she stammered. "Shouldn't you get back?"

Zekki remained motionless, pink nose flushed with excitement. "I hear something moving. If I could just . . ." Tentatively he bumped the screen door with his head, starting back as it creaked, shuddered, then swung open.

Dazzling summer light hurt their eyes, and the cats gaped in wonderment as a water bug shambled across the welcome mat and a lizard slithered up a pot of flowers.

"What are you waiting for?" The silky voice sounded close, floating from somewhere above, and as if performing a dance rehearsed their whole lives, Zekki and Pris slid through the doorway and into the Outs at last.

Zekki and Pris stood together only inches beyond the screen, staring at the vastness of this new frontier. Two huge potted ferns stood on either side of the door, and the cats crouched wide-eyed between lush fronds, observing the porch. A row of holly bushes separated the veranda from the front yard, and terra-cotta planters, overflowing with red geraniums, marched down three rows of steps leading to a driveway.

"Welcome to paradise."

Whirling at the sound, they peered through the cascading vegetation and gasped.

Draped across the porch swing, one paw dangling off the slatted wooden seat, was the most amazing cat they'd ever seen.

Zekki hissed instinctively, blue eyes dilated to black, while Pris leaped backward, turned in midair, and dashed behind a flowerpot.

Ignoring their reaction, the stranger stretched, and with one fluid movement leaped to the ground. He was gray and huge, fully six inches taller than the stocky Zekki or the plump calico, with dark tiger stripes forming an M over a sloping, lion-like nose. But the most startling thing about him was his eyes—or, more accurately, his eye, for where his right eye should have been, only a scarred and sunken slit remained. The left one, however, was clear, intelligent, and piercing. It was the eye of a warrior, and the white cat watched in paralyzed fascination as the creature glided forward, his remaining eye unblinking. "I'm a friend, remember?"

Zekki nodded, wondering why he found the statement troubling.

Peering toward the geraniums, the big male cocked his head. "And who do we have here, I wonder?"

Pris peeked from behind the pot. "Hello," she squeaked.

"Come out and let's take a look at you, my dear." He advanced with a grace that seemed strange, considering his size.

Slinking from her hiding place, the calico froze, her amber eyes frightened and huge.

"Her name's Pris." The white cat quickly placed himself between the quivering calico and the stranger. "I'm Zekki."

The tom tilted his head, dipping and swaying for a better look, then abruptly stalked to the welcome mat, tenderly scratching his wounded socket against the rattan weaving. "You can call me Jett."

In the distance a dog barked, and the chatter of talk radio drifted from a neighboring window.

"So!" Jett sat down. "What would you two like to do?"

"Do?" repeated Pris.

"You've never been out before, have you?"

The two cats shook their heads.

"Then let's take a little tour of the neighborhood."

"That would be great!" Pris squealed. "I've always wondered if—"

"Thanks," Zekki interrupted, pushing her toward the door and feeling an overwhelming and surprising urge to get back inside. "But actually this probably isn't a good day for that."

"It isn't?" the calico said with genuine bewilderment.

"No." Zekki grunted, pushing Pris across the porch. "I mean, Buddy and The Boy will be back soon, and we should be in the house before then."

Jett's eye brightened with innocent interest. "Buddy?"

"Yes, he lives here, too," Pris chimed in. "He's a cat. Older . . . gone to the vet's."

"I see." Jett shrugged. "Well, of course, if you don't want to do anything, it's up to you, but I did catch a squirrel this morning; stashed it a couple of blocks down, and I thought maybe . . . no, no, of course, never mind, you need to go back." His voice trailed off, and he stared with sudden interest at the flowerpot where the hapless lizard lay frozen beneath a leaf.

Zekki's heart pounded. He'd only seen squirrels from windows, tails flicking with insolence, black eyes mocking and rude. Never in his wildest dreams had he expected to touch one.

"You mean a *real* squirrel? Tail, feet, and everything?" Pris's nose flushed with excitement.

"Oh, yes, the whole thing. But never mind." Walking to the geraniums, the gray cat glared pointedly into the pot, then continued down the steps. "It was nice meeting you."

"Wait!" Zekki shrieked. How many times had he longed for this moment? Yesterday, just touching grass was beyond his dreams, and now, the Outs lay before him, verdant, fragrant, ripe for exploration. He turned toward the calico. "Shouldn't we just take a quick look? I mean, just a look, that's all."

"I don't know . . . what about" she lowered her voice "The Cat Master? We always said if we got out, we'd look for him."

Jett's ear scoped in her direction. "Did you say, 'The Cat Master'?"

"Yes," Pris, said. "We've always wanted to meet—"

"It's just a game we play," the white cat interrupted. "Buddy told us no cat can actually find him."

"I hate to disagree with your friend, but that's not true." Jett nonchalantly licked his hind leg. "I happen to know The Cat Master well."

"You do?" Zekki was stunned. He'd always assumed Buddy knew everything.

Jett smiled. "I can prove it if you don't believe me. He's in the area. If the two of you would like an introduction . . . but, of course . . . no, no . . . you really should stay here." He turned to leave, his thick striped tail floating over his back as though suspended by invisible wires.

"No, wait, we're coming, we're coming!" Zekki skidded across the porch and down the three steps. He caught up with Jett by the driveway and was about to follow him onto the sidewalk, when Pris's plaintive voice called from the porch.

"What about Buddy?"

Zekki slammed to a halt, ears pulsing with stress.

Jett continued walking.

"Could you maybe wait up? We've got a little problem."

The big cat glided to a halt. "And what could that be?"

"We can't leave." Zekki's voice shook with disappointment. "Our friend's gone, and he won't know what's happened to us if we leave."

"Not to worry." Jett smiled with friendly tolerance. "I can fix that." In three giant leaps he bounded up the steps and padded to the door. With a jaunty wink, he backed to the screen, flicked his tail, and proceeded to direct a hard stream of urine directly against the wire. "There, that should do it." He clawed the mat with satisfaction. "I think that'll tell your friend what's happened."

The young cats stood in shock.

"What do you think you're doing?" Pris screamed, hurling herself toward the door. "That's not a box! Where's your litter box?" Frantically, she covered the offending puddle with dust, leaves, and air.

Zekki stared at the dripping liquid. "That was, that was . . . what *was* that?"

"Think of it as a little note for your friend that Mother will deliver." Jett playfully swatted Pris's flank, and she batted back with a dainty paw. "This way." He rubbed against Zekki, his big body almost knocking him down. "Buddy knows exactly where you are in case he wants to find you."

In one smooth motion, Jett leaped over the holly bushes, hopped stiff-legged through the grass, then whirled into a crouch, tail slapping the ground. "And now, my friends," he hissed, eye gleaming in the sunlight, "who's for adventure?"

FIVE

THE LIZARD PEERED OUT from the geraniums, heart still pounding with alarm.

Excited chatter faded in the distance, and he could barely see the three cats as they trotted single file down the sidewalk, finally disappearing around a corner.

Drawing a shaky breath, he carefully slithered from the pot, scurrying toward the crawl space. The big tom had seen him. There was no mistaking that. So why had he been spared? Not only that, but it appeared all the cats were now gone. Eyes blinking rapidly, the lizard furrowed his brow. He'd always been lucky, but this was remarkable even for him.

Vaguely he wondered if perhaps there was a deeper meaning, something he hadn't considered. The idea was so foreign he ignored it and went straight to his favorite conclusion: He deserved it. After all, there was an order to the universe: lizard on top, everything else on the bottom. You couldn't argue with the truth, he thought, crawling up the bricks and heading for the grate. The truth never lied.

• • •

Classical music drifted from the radio, and the car's engine droned and hummed.

Bracing his legs, Buddy tried not to fall as the carrier bumped and shifted in the back seat. Mrs. O'Connell turned the steering wheel sharply, and the yellow tom was engulfed in waves of vertigo ending in full-blown nausea as the automobile rocked to a stop.

The carrier was hoisted from the car, and Buddy struggled to keep his footing on the slippery plastic as it bounced against The Boy's legs. After a short walk a door squeaked open, and he was assaulted by the unmistakable scent of urine, disinfectant, and fear. Instantly he recognized the veterinarian's clinic, a place he'd been to only once but had never forgotten.

The carrier thumped on the floor, and Mrs. O'Connell spoke to someone about an appointment. In the distance cages rattled, identification tags jingled on collars, and animals whined and keened in pain and confusion. Buddy's heartbeat quickened. What if they kept him here, just when Zekki and Pris needed him most? Panicked, he whirled in the cramped enclosure, yowling in distress.

"It's okay." The Boy pulled him from the box, arranging him on bony knees. Gratefully, Buddy rubbed the familiar hand, noticing that his anxiety was fading.

The waiting room was air-conditioned, and someone had turned the temperature too low in reaction to the blistering Texas afternoon. Shivering, Buddy surveyed his surroundings. Chairs lined the pale green walls, and a tangle of pet postings was displayed on a corkboard by the door. Across from The Boy a woman chattered on a cell phone while her obese Pekinese snorted and huffed in her arms. To her right a man cuddled something in a fluffy towel. Occasionally he would peer into the bundle, mumbling soft, soothing sounds to the round form beneath.

Settling against The Boy, Buddy watched with interest as the towel began to move.

Alarmed, the man placed his hands around the undulating form and shifted the entire bundle to his chest, but the wriggling continued. Suddenly, with a determined thrust of its head, the creature emerged from the folds of fabric, stretched seductively, and stared straight into Buddy's eyes.

The tom felt a dramatic shift in temperature. His heart rate slowed to a feeble flutter, then abruptly accelerated to a wild and furious pounding.

Sitting serenely before him, periwinkle eyes glittering with intelligence, was the most beautiful feline he had ever seen. Her delicate body was creamy white, with face, ears, paws, and tail a smoky taupe. The head was aristocratic and narrow, and a gold collar with a tiny silver bell encircled her throat like a serpent. Hypnotic eyes squeezed shut in silent greeting, then opened wide. "What a relief," she sighed. "I was suffocating in there."

For a moment Buddy stopped breathing altogether. Was it possible she was speaking to him? He blinked, he sat up, he sat down, he heard angels singing.

"My name's Shan Dara." She shook her head, the little

bell tinkling merrily against her milky throat. "And yours?"

His name! She'd asked his name! Inhaling deeply, he opened his mouth, managed a garbled "Buddy," and choked on a hair ball. It was unbelievable, humiliating, and so typical of this miserable day.

The Boy quickly placed him on the floor, and after much gagging and retching, no hair ball appeared. He remained hunched on the linoleum, staring at a crumpled brochure that read, "Neuter and Spay: Do It Today!"

"Easy, Bud," The Boy said, gently massaging his throat. "You're okay."

"This isn't possible," Buddy thought, fighting an irresistible urge to back under the chair and sit there until he grew old, died, and turned to dust. "This never, ever happens to me," he finally managed to mumble. "I mean this is just so unusual." Ashamed to look up, he licked his paw with embarrassment. "Seriously." He knew he was babbling but couldn't seem to stop. "Has that ever happened to you? I mean one minute you're fine and then the next . . ." He managed a crooked smile he hoped was winning and willed himself to look into what he hoped would be the compassionate blue eyes of the goddess.

Instead, the bulging brown eyes of the Pekinese stared back. The dog snorted with contempt. "He paid, she's gone, and you're disgusting."

"Gone?" His pulse fluttered like a pinned butterfly. "Where?"

The dog looked toward the street. "Out there."

Through the picture window Buddy could see a dark-gray vehicle slowly backing away from the curb. An elegant face with periwinkle eyes watched from the window, an engine revved, and she was gone.

Asphalt shimmered in the heat, and a wasp zoomed against the glass, then dropped to the sidewalk. Buddy felt a pang of empathy that quickly turned to fear at the sight of the veterinarian's assistant. She was a wiry young woman with *I Love Daryl* tattooed on her wrist. In one motion she scooped him from the floor and carried him into the examining room.

Buddy thrashed in her grip and almost escaped before he was hurled onto a metal table.

Twisting his head at a bone-crunching angle, she held him by the nape of his neck, immobilized and helpless.

"You don't have to do that!" The Boy's voice was high pitched with anger. "He's not mean or anything."

The girl's grip tightened, and Buddy felt a sudden compassion for the unfortunate Daryl.

"It's okay," she drawled, cracking gum and yanking him closer. "I've got him."

The vet entered the room and commented on how well Buddy looked since his rescue. She listened patiently to the O'Connells' concerns, gave Buddy a brief exam that proved normal, and administered a mild sedative by injection.

Buddy winced, a dog howled forlornly from the kennel, and outside in the empty waiting room, a tiny silver bell lay silently beneath a chair.

S I X

BUDDY SAT ON THE BOY'S LAP gazing at the dashboard of the car. The sedative had left him languid and weak, and he watched in wonder as pair after pair of periwinkle eyes marched in dreamy procession before his face.

The car stopped, and Mrs. O'Connell leaned over and patted The Boy's knee. "Honey, I don't think we need to put Buddy in the carrier just to get him into the house. Why don't you hold him until I come around and open your door?"

Choruses of cicadas droned in the heat as the cat settled with groggy detachment into The Boy's arms.

A waft of hot air blew a leaf, some dust, and a clump of silky white fur through the open window. Buddy's eyes focused on the hair with difficulty as it floated in a beam of sunlight, hung for a moment, then drifted onto The Boy's thigh where it stuck. The fur seemed familiar, and something about its presence in the car was disturbing. The tom struggled to identify the feeling, but the sun was so warm and comfortable he lost interest, deciding to rest his chin against The Boy's thumb instead. A strand of the white hair tickled his nose, and shaking his head, he closed his eyes.

"So far, so good," The Boy said, gently inching him higher against his shoulder and easing himself from the car.

Buddy snuggled close as they stopped by the geranium pots, waiting as Mrs. O'Connell checked the mailbox. A friendly scent rose from the flowers. Twitching his nose Buddy identified the smell. No problem; it was only Pris. Something shifted in the back of his brain.

Pris's scent on the porch.

White fur blowing into the car.

Buddy's eyes snapped open and warning bells tolled deep in his head. Something was wrong.

"Oh my gosh!" Mrs. O'Connell said with surprise. "The door's open!"

Something was terribly wrong.

The Boy walked forward, and an acrid stench, strong with ammonia and unmistakably familiar, assaulted Buddy's senses. Jett! Zekki and Pris were out! Jett had taken them!

The Boy's hand reached toward the door, and the cat strained upward, bracing his hind legs against the thin arm and pushing as hard as he could. With a grunt he catapulted into space, twisted in a desperate attempt for equilibrium, then crashed into the bushes.

The O'Connells seemed to be moving in slow motion.

"Buddy!" The Boy cried.

"Ow!" His mother shrieked, stumbling over the cat carrier and cracking her knee on a potted fern as she fell.

Buddy thrashed in the foliage, dimly aware of The Boy helping his mother to her feet and into the house. Rolling from beneath the prickly leaves, Buddy wobbled toward the backyard, desperate for a place to hide until he could think clearly again.

A door slammed, and The Boy's footsteps thumped down the steps. "Buddy! Here, Pris. Here, Zek!"

Things you love will suffer.

Buddy staggered to the patio, finally collapsing against the air conditioner.

Something rustled, and he turned to see a lizard's face peering from a vent that led underneath the house. Near it was a small screen that had somehow pulled loose and lay rusting in the leaves.

Startled, the creature mouthed an obscenity and darted back inside.

The Boy's footsteps pounded closer.

Shutting his eyes and praying he wouldn't get stuck, Buddy dove through the opening, plummeting into a void of black.

For a moment he felt disoriented and sick. Still light-headed, he blinked and looked around.

The place was amazingly cool, considering the summer heat, and cobwebs iced with dust drifted in fuzzy strands from the low ceiling. The crawl space was littered with things left after the addition was built many years before. A soiled workman's cap lay amid fragmented candy wrappers, and a dented coffee can was filled with cigarette butts, nails, and screws.

The cat coughed. Thirst scorched his throat, and his

head bobbed and shook as the effects of the tranquilizer began to dissipate.

From outside, the frenzied searching and desperate calls for the cats continued.

Buddy's heart ached. With a sigh, he crept from the vent and lay down, resting his head on the dusty cap.

The cap moved.

Buddy lurched to his feet, ears forward and alert.

It moved again, and instinctively he pinned it with a well-aimed paw.

"You're on my tail!" a muffled voice screamed. Something squirmed and twisted beneath the brim, and slowly a small, gray head appeared; amber eyes blinked with fury. "Go ahead, kill me!" it shrieked. "It was bound to happen eventually!"

Surprised, Buddy moved back. "I don't eat lizards," he managed to mumble before collapsing to the ground in a woozy heap.

The lizard started to run, then stopped, watching the cat intently. Could this be the one they'd taken to the vet? It definitely looked sick, maybe it was even dying. The thought was very appealing. Carefully the lizard ventured from beneath the cap, feeling for the second time that day that some higher power might be at work. "I didn't say 'eat,'" he noted with patronizing sarcasm. "I said 'kill.'" There was no response from the cat, and sensing he wasn't in immediate danger, the lizard dove back beneath the hat, voice alternately loud and muffled as he poked his head in and out.

"When are you guys gonna learn they don't like reptiles

in the house? Can you remember the last time a human said, 'Thanks for the dead thing, leave it on the bed'?" He pulled himself from under the brim, something clutched in his spiny toes. "Look at this, just look at this!"

The cat raised a wobbly head. "What is it?"

"What is it?" he screamed. "It's only my tail, that's all! You just pulled my tail off!" Throwing it in the dirt, he gestured with fury. "Take a look, pal! It was one of the best I ever had!" With a hitching sob he picked up the neatly snapped appendage and clamored onto the hat.

Buddy attempted to stand, then sat down. "Who are you?"

"Orie," the lizard spat, picturing the cat dead.

"I'm Buddy, and I—I'm sorry about the tail." The tom staggered to his feet, moving slowly toward the vent. "I didn't know you were there."

The Boy's frantic voice drifted from the street. "Here kitty! Bud! Zekki! Here Pris!"

"A little under the weather?" the lizard asked, feeling cocky and loose.

Buddy stared into the dark, ignoring him.

Jumping from the hat, the lizard swaggered closer. "Because of all the cats I've seen today, and believe me, it's been a regular cat convention out there, you look the worse." He was definitely on a roll and fantasized he was holding a microphone. *So did you hear the one about the dying kitty? Take my tail, PLEEESE!* It was such an amusing thought, he actually laughed out loud.

The tabby whirled. "You've seen other cats today?"

Startled, the lizard jumped. Perhaps he'd misjudged the cat's affliction. "Yeah, yeah, I saw a couple," he whispered, inching toward the shelter of the coffee can.

Buddy crept closer, whiskers forward, eyes focused and clear. "Did you see a white cat with long fur and a short-haired calico?"

"You know, I think I did." Orie peddled backward, stunned by a horrible revelation: This cat was definitely not dying! Tripping on a candy wrapper, he crashed into the coffee can, which slowly tipped, spilling nails and cigarette butts onto his back. "And there was another one, too." He choked, shaking ashes from his snout.

Buddy blinked. "What other one?"

"Look, I'll make you a deal, okay?" Orie warbled, suddenly aware that a washer had landed on his head where it balanced like a designer chapeau.

The cat remained motionless, watching.

"I'll tell you everything I know about those cats and the big gray one, and you don't kill me." He tried to look shrewd and in control as the washer slid forward, dangling over one eye. "Is that a deal?"

The tom's tail whipped furiously in the dirt. "The only thing I'm interested in is what you saw."

Dust puffed into the dry air, and the lizard's eyes began to burn and water. "I'm telling you, I hardly know anything." His nose started to run, and he sneezed. "I was minding my own business up in the flowerpot, and suddenly these two cats walked out of the house." He looked hopefully at Buddy. "Anyway, they started talking to this big gray tabby." Orie sneezed again. "And then they all walked away together. Boom. That's it, end of story."

Buddy inched closer. "You didn't hear anything?"

Orie wiped a dripping snout on his foreleg. "No, I mean, yeah, yeah, they said something about going to see a cat master, finding squirrels, stuff like that. I swear that's all I know." Exhausted, he collapsed in a heap, head flopped forward, nose in the dirt. "This is where you kill me, right?"

"I already told you I'm not going to eat you," Buddy said.

The lizard stared in amazement, washer sliding from his head. "You mean . . . that's all?"

"Yes, that's all."

Above them, pacing footsteps and worried voices drifted through the crawl space, their sad echoes mingling with a distant freight train's piercing whistle.

Buddy listened, body sagging with fatigue. "I don't want to talk anymore." With a ragged sigh, he lay by the vent, face to the wall.

"Sure, no problem. Hard day, everybody's tired," Orie croaked, scurrying away before the cat changed his mind and ate him just for kicks. Shaking with relief, he clamored onto the cap and squinted into the darkness. Was it possible his life had been spared *again*? But why? Orie tapped the nails of one claw, trying to remember any particular kindness or acts of bravery he'd performed that could account for such a miracle. There weren't any. He shrugged. Apparently things like this didn't apply to him, though perhaps he should perform a good deed some day just to make sure. He furrowed his brow in concentration. So why hadn't the cats eaten him? There could only be one answer: He was too special to die!

Burrowing into the cloth, he squirmed with joy. There was a higher power at work, its intentions unknown but welcome. "I'm special," he intoned, trembling at the enormity of such a revelation. Wiping his snout on the greasy fabric, he laughed and wept, thanking providence for his newly discovered calling and burning with a righteous fire only the newly converted truly understand.

SEVEN

ZEKKI AND PRIS lay entwined on the sparse, dry grass, their breathing steady and deep.

In contrast, Jett had chosen a more concealed area beneath a bush where he slept in a tight ball, front paws tucked beneath his body, head bowed and almost touching his chest.

They had traveled many blocks since leaving the O'Connells, and the two young cats had been difficult to control. Their childish enthusiasm was annoying, and it had been almost impossible to drag them away from the squirrel's remains. Insisting on a few hours' rest, Jett had led them behind an abandoned doghouse, where exhausted and elated, they'd immediately fallen asleep.

A dove flapped on a sycamore branch, wings whistling, and Jett jerked awake. A lemony moon glowed against the summer sky. Digging his claws into a spray of crabgrass, he sighed with satisfaction. Zekki and Pris were obviously unaware that the old Master was dead, which probably meant that Buddy was unaware, too. The telepathic interference had worked! Jett smirked with pride. It was all happening as planned. So smooth, so easy, so stupidly simple. The young cats were his, and all that remained was for Buddy to come to their rescue. Yawning, he assessed his sleeping companions. The male was a typical "pretty boy," all long white hair, blue eyes and prissy pink ears, nose and pads. The female, on the other hand, was very appealing in an overstuffed way. Round head and eyes, small ears set high, and a coat perfectly marked with ginger, white, and black. Unfortunately not even good looks could disguise Indoor inferiority, and these two were particularly dull with none of the edgy intellect of Ferals. Jett frowned, unpleasant memories fighting for attention. As passive as Buddy appeared, he must never be underestimated . . . *like before*. Never mind, Jett consoled himself. The new plan was much more sophisticated without the recklessness of youth. This time, cunning and manipulation would prevail, and Jett was a master at both. With a grunt of resolution, he strode to the cats and nipped Zekki's hind leg. "Get up!"

Both animals jumped, scuttling to a crouched position.

"What's wrong?" Zekki's words slurred with confusion.

"Nothing's wrong. It's just time to leave."

Pris yawned. "But we just went to sleep a minute ago."

"You're in the Outs now, my dear." He rubbed his itching scar against her flank. "Where sleep is a gift, not a given."

Pris shrank at the touch, her face a mixture of fear and revulsion.

Her rebuke stung, and Jett fought an old feeling of shame. "She would pay for that kind of disrespect," he thought, fading into the shadows. "They would all pay."

The calico sidled closer to Zekki. "I think I want to go home."

Cocking his head in puzzlement, the white cat frowned. "Why? We've only been out a little while."

"I don't know. It's sort of scary out here, and I miss The Boy and Buddy . . . and I—I . . ." Her little chin trembled. "I miss our home!"

"Did I hear someone say 'home'?" Jett's voice crackled from the darkness.

Both animals tensed, and Zekki took a deep breath. "Yes, sir. Pris wants to go—"

"Oh, but why?" Jett interrupted, trotting into the light and sitting with a thump. He turned his weeping scar toward them in a pitiful picture of despair. "Haven't you had a good time? Didn't I keep my word about the squirrel?" A rivulet of moisture oozed from the empty socket and rolled like a teardrop along the side of his nose and through his luxurious whiskers. "Is it something I've done?"

The young cats shifted uncomfortably.

"No, sir, it's nothing like that, it's just . . ." Zekki stumbled for words.

The creature was so ridiculous, stuttering and straining to be polite, that Jett wanted to laugh. "Then what is it?"

"Well, Pris is . . . well, Pris feels . . . well, she's a girl, sir," Zekki finally sputtered, giving a huge sigh of relief and looking toward the calico for approval.

She thwacked him in the head, her rotund body trembling with indignation. "That's not why I want to go home!"

Zekki squeaked with surprise.

"Of course it isn't," Jett crooned, giving a sympathetic nod to the calico. "I just think you're homesick." He moved closer, noting with satisfaction that this time she didn't shrink away. "Could that be it, just some old-fashioned homesickness?" He licked her ear with friendly reassurance.

"Maybe a little." She relaxed, dipping her head shyly. "But if we did decide we'd like to go, that would be okay, wouldn't it?"

"Absolutely! Feel free to take off anytime you want." Raising a hind leg, Jett scratched the back of his head. "You shouldn't have any trouble finding your way home, especially since you've both been marking a trail." The hind leg stopped in mid-scratch, his great paw rising behind him like a war feather. He stared expectedly at the stricken faces before him. "You have been marking a . . . oh dear, you haven't been?" Lowering his leg, he squinted at the ground in deep concentration. "Well, luckily, I've been marking here and there, and I think with Mother's help, I can get us back." His eye glistened with friendly confidence. "Yes, I'm almost sure I can."

The young cats sighed with relief.

"Gee, that's great, you sure think of everything." Zekki nodded with earnest admiration.

"I try," Jett murmured. "I certainly try." Inhaling the thick night air, he looked at the graying sky. Dawn was very close, they still had miles to go, and he felt an urgency to leave. "Of course we still haven't seen The Cat Master. So, do you want to go home or continue on?" He tried to look indifferent. "I think He'd be very interested in meeting you."

"He would?" said Zekki.

"Why wouldn't he? You strike me as extremely intelligent cats."

The young tom glowed with importance. "How about it, Pris? Don't you think we should keep going? We'll never get this chance again, and Jett said he'd take us home whenever we want."

"Okay," she said reluctantly. "We'll see The Cat Master, and then we'll go home, right?"

"Right," Jett said. "An excellent plan. So, everyone rested and ready?"

The cats nodded.

"Then follow me." Without a backward glance, he leaped the cyclone fence behind the doghouse and bounded into the alley.

Zekki followed first, encouraging the calico as she struggled to the top and dropped awkwardly to the other side.

"Where exactly are we going?" she panted, darting after Jett's shadowy figure.

"I don't know. Who cares? We're in the Outs! We're free! We can do anything we want!"

Pris stopped, eyes sad. "But what about Buddy? He doesn't know where we are or if we're okay."

"He'll understand," Zekki said, twitching with discomfort. "This is the adventure of a lifetime, right? Buddy wouldn't want us to miss The Cat Master. I mean, it's probably historic!" He nudged the calico's head. "We'll see Buddy again soon and tell him all about it, I promise."

Jett waited a few yards ahead, watching impatiently as the animals stumbled through the darkness. "If you're coming, keep up; it's dangerous here."

49

A motorcycle rumbled through an intersection, and the cats hid behind a tangle of brambles as it zoomed by. They continued on through the brush, thorns tearing their coats and scratching their ears and noses. Zekki turned to clean a trickle of blood from the calico's ear.

"When I want you to stop, I'll tell you." Jett's voice was cold. Suddenly subdued, the young cats followed him across two side streets and into another alleyway.

The light was dimmer in this stretch of block, and the houses were even more dilapidated. Garbage cans were piled high with trash, and some had turned over, their contents rotting in the dirt. Rats scuttled behind weeds, and Zekki attempted to chase one as it made its way along the fence line.

"No hunting. Not now." Jett growled.

Pris pushed her nose into an empty carton. "But I'm hungry."

"We'll eat later." Jett's manner was increasingly agitated, and without warning, he tensed, eye scanning the alley, ears flattened against his skull.

The cats crouched, tails barely flicking.

A sudden banging broke the silence. Two trash cans tipped into the dirt, their lids twirling like tops before clanging to the ground.

Zekki and Pris scaled a scraggly crepe myrtle, and Jett sprang into the bushes, fur bushed like a halo around his head.

"Who is it, who's there?" a terrified voice screeched.

Jett slithered forward, muscles bulging, ready to strike.

The young cats clung to the tree, watching in horrified

silence at the scene below. Already a big cat, Jett now seemed huge, demonic, like something that had pretended to be feline and was now stripped of its mask, standing naked in its true form. A moaning growl came from his throat, and his tail snapped the ground like a whip. "Come out!" he yowled. "Come out now, before I kill you!"

"Jett?" the voice floated somewhere in the gloom. "Is that you?"

"I said come out!"

With a squeak of panic, a black form tumbled from the bin, rolling submissively in the dirt. "Don't hurt me. It's Soot! It's Soot!"

Jett stared at the writhing form. "Soot?" He laughed, his voice once more even and smooth. "Why didn't you say so?"

The black cat slowly righted itself and hunched in the dirt. Emaciated, with wild copper eyes and short dry fur, his tail was crooked as though broken, and one ear drooped, lopsided and floppy. "Thought it was you, Jett, but, but I wasn't sure," he muttered.

Pris and Zekki clamored to the ground, heads cocked with curiosity.

Startled, the stranger darted against the fence, hissing.

"Oh, don't worry about them," Jett crooned, mask back in place. "They're new friends, very peaceful, no danger."

Soot gave a shaky sigh, and the gray tom blinked his eye as though struggling to pierce the darkness. "So, where is Ahn-ya?" Jett asked.

"She—she's down about a block in a cardboard box."

"And the kittens?" Jett said, pride softening his voice.

The Feral stared blankly at the ground. "They're with her."

"Well, come on, then." With a merry flick of his thick tail, Jett trotted down the alley, once again cocky and assured.

Pris and Zekki scurried behind, gazing shyly at the newcomer as they passed, and Soot followed, slinking close to the fence.

The alley was congested, with rusted auto parts, discarded sinks, and plastic bags spewing decaying refuse in all directions. Jett maneuvered through the obstacles with casual gracefulness.

"There it is," Soot called.

The cats stopped near a large cardboard box. Splotched with dirt and mildew, it lay on its side, the opening squashed against a metal trash bin.

The young cats kept a respectful distance as Jett sauntered to the carton. "Ahn-ya, it's me. I've come to see the kittens."

At first it seemed that Soot had been mistaken; that the box was empty, but finally a faint rustle came from somewhere inside, and a dim form slowly appeared at the opening. She was a wiry tortoiseshell, and her movements were slow and stiff as she came toward them. Pushing a delicate head against the big tom's chest, she sat heavily at his feet. "Jett," she said quietly.

"I've come to see our kittens," he answered, rubbing his face along her shoulders and neck. Suddenly he stepped back as though confused. "But where is everyone?"

She tilted her head, and a streetlight illuminated eyes that were matted and dull. "They're all dead, except for Soot and me."

Jett stared at her ravished face for the first time. "What's wrong with you?" His mouth twisted in horror, and he staggered back. "You're diseased!"

Puffy clouds drifted across the moon momentarily obscuring her face, and her ragged breathing filled the night in wordless answer.

"No!" The big tom's anguished wail reverberated through the alley, and he whirled with fury on Soot. "Don't come near me," he hissed, flattening his ears, paw raised to strike. "You're all diseased!"

"No, no, I'm not sick! I'm okay, honest!"

Jett recoiled. "So you say."

"But where are the kittens?" Pris stretched her neck toward the female sitting silently in the dirt.

"They're in the box." Ahn-ya gave a wet cough, bony shoulders heaving with the effort, and struggled to her feet. "All of our litters . . . all of the colony . . . all dead." With shaky dignity, she turned toward the cardboard box, slender tail dragging behind. Reaching the opening, she paused. "All dead," she repeated; then she vanished without a sound.

Jett hunched beneath the crepe myrtle, eye fixed and unblinking on the spot where Ahn-ya had been. "All dead," he enunciated carefully. An avalanche of emotion tore through his mind. The colony had been destroyed by disease, and now his kittens were gone, his lineage broken, and Ahn-ya was . . . A coil of grief constricted his chest, but he stopped it with a shake of his head. Feelings were bad—dangerous, and not to be tolerated. Scorching pain pulsed behind his socket, and he grimaced. "Never mind," he thought, squinting against the relentless ache. Just a little more time, a little more planning, and every wrong would be righted. All he had to do was lure Buddy into the Outs and expose him at The Gathering. After that, it would be plain to all that Jett was the rightful successor. A light breeze rustled the foliage, and he lifted his head. "Bring me his scent, Mother," he intoned, blocking all memories of Ahn-ya's ravaged face. "Soon they'll all know I'm the one." Perfected by years of practice, the sense of loss dissipated, replaced by something cruel, cold, and irreversible. "The punishment has only begun," he muttered and noticed with satisfaction the pain had completely gone.

Zekki moved tentatively toward the box.

"You shouldn't go in there." Soot cringed, haunches quivering.

"It's okay," Pris said with confidence. "We've had vaccinations."

"Vaccinations?"

Shifting with impatience, Zekki snorted. "You know, humans stick you with needles, and it keeps you from getting sick."

Soot drew a quick breath. "You mean, you're *Indoors*?" He emphasized the word as though referring to royalty.

"Oh, yes." The calico touched his ebony nose with hers. "We live in a house and everything." She crept to Jett's motionless form, keeping a watchful distance. "Are we going to stay here?"

"No." Moving from the bush, Jett brushed past. "I'll never come here again." For one brief moment he paused by the box, body stiff, eye staring straight ahead; then, with star-tling power, he vaulted the fence into an adjoining yard.

Dawn shimmered through the alley, and the three remaining cats blinked with confusion.

"It was nice meeting you, Soot." Pris craned her neck, eager to follow. "But we'd better go."

"Can I come?" Soot whispered. "I don't even care where you're going. I just need to get out of here."

"I—I don't know." She looked at Zekki. "Can he?"

"I'm not sick, I swear I'm not!" Creeping closer the black cat twisted his head, voice desperate and pleading. "But the alley is contaminated. If I don't leave now, I'll end up like the rest."

Zekki anxiously licked his chops. "Well . . . I mean Jett didn't say you couldn't."

Soot inched forward, eyes round and hopeful.

"Okay, okay, but both of you hurry!" With one quick movement Zekki dashed for the fence and jumped over it. The others quickly followed.

Running in single file, they wound through yards and alleys, finally reaching Jett who was waiting beneath a mail-box.

They traveled the rest of the way in silence, Jett striding in machinelike precision down streets and pathways, Zekki and Pris racing to keep up, and the black cat scurrying a dis-creet distance behind.

Lights blinked on in the neighborhoods, the sounds of slamming car doors and blaring TV weather reports signaling another workday.

Just as the morning sun filtered through the trees, Jett led the panting trio to a ramshackle shed, where he squeezed behind a rusted lawn mower.

Paws blistered and throbbing, Zekki and Pris collapsed beneath a workbench, and Soot curled up in an empty flowerpot, his wasted body twitching with exhaustion.

The morning sun shone in the alleyway, and a garbage truck lurched along, unloading the contents of dumpsters and trash cans into its cavernous mouth.

A sweaty young man ran alongside the vehicle, swinging plastic bags and newspapers up to his partner who made sure nothing spilled out of the churning machine. In the next block the man noticed a lone cardboard box leaning against a dumpster. Bending down as they passed, he tossed it into the air and onto the truck with one motion. Light as a feather, it seemed to hang for a split second, suspended in the sunlight, and then tumbled quietly into the yawning darkness below.

EIGHT

BUDDY AWOKE, STARTLED AND AFRAID. At first he couldn't remember where he was and began a frantic search for The Boy. Reality zoomed back in one queasy jolt, and he stood in the crawl space forcing himself to be calm.

The vet's sedative had worn off, but his head hurt and his tongue was parched and thick. Stiff from the fall in the bushes, he limped to where the lizard lay sleeping and tried to decide the best way to wake him. Finally, he cleared his throat.

Orie, who now rested against the wall, emitted a gurgled snore and pushed his snout further under one clawed foot.

Buddy cleared his throat again, and the reptile jumped, eyes wide and terrified.

"What? What's going on?" he shrieked.

"Everything's fine, take it easy." Buddy moved back, hoping to give the frightened creature a sense of safety. "I have to get out of here, and I need to ask you some questions. Are you awake?"

"I am totally awake. I've been awake for hours." Orie blinked rapidly and scrambled to his feet. "What?"

"I need some water. Where can I get some?"

The lizard frowned, reached one clawed foot behind his body as if searching for something, then froze. Swiveling his neck, he stared at his back. "It's gone!" he screamed. "It's gone, gone—!"

"Calm down! Stop!" Buddy interrupted. "It's okay, everything's all right. Your tail sort of got . . . broken off, remember? I think you put it under the cap."

Orie gaped, sides heaving with emotion. "Right, right, I knew that."

Oak leaves rattled against the grate, and the two animals sat in an uneasy quietness.

"I also need something to eat," Buddy finally said. "I'm hungry but not picky. Anything will do at this point."

The lizard looked alarmed.

"No, no," Buddy said. "I was telling the truth last night, I really wouldn't eat . . . you know . . ." His voice trailed off. "You."

Orie's eyes narrowed with cunning. "So . . . if I help you find food and stuff, would that be considered an act of"— his lip curled with disgust—"kindness? Like a good deed?"

"A good deed?" Buddy repeated, feeling confused. "I guess you could call it that."

"Then this is your lucky day, pal," Orie said. "Because I've been looking for one of those." Abruptly, he scuttled to the vent and looked into the yard, brow creased with con- centration. "You can get some food next door, but we've got to go *now*." With one glance at the cat, he scrambled through the opening and vanished into the yard.

Pushing himself through the grate, Buddy stopped for a moment beneath the den window. The house seemed quiet, and he wondered if Mrs. O'Connell was letting The Boy sleep. "That's okay," he murmured, slinking through the foliage. "Once I find Zekki and Pris, we'll all come back here, and things will be exactly like they were before." But he knew this wasn't true, even if he didn't exactly know why.

Orie waited nervously on the patio. The stump where his tail had once been twitched from side to side. He gestured toward a chain-link fence separating the O'Connells' property from their neighbor's. "There's some food up there on that deck," he hissed in a stage whisper, "and water in a bowl by the birdbath."

Buddy licked his chops. He hadn't eaten or drunk anything in twenty-four hours, and he felt dehydrated and weak. Wiggling closer to the fence, he strained to see. The lizard was right. There was food on a deck by the back door, and the birdbath stood in a graceful circle of ferns in the yard. "Thanks, Orie, I won't forget this."

"Good," the lizard replied. "There's one thing, though."

"What's that?" Buddy called as he vaulted over the fence and slunk toward the steps.

"You should probably watch out for the dog."

Buddy whirled and froze. "The dog?" Of course! Why hadn't he remembered? He had always heard barking from this direction, but the O'Connell's bushes were so thick, he'd never been able to see anything.

"Don't worry, it's too early for her to be out." Orie squinted into the sky. "Yeah, I'm sure it's not time for her to be . . ."

The back door of the porch burst open, and a large German shepherd lumbered onto the deck.

"Out," Orie finished weakly.

Panicked, Buddy sank into the grass, sheltered by a hedge of azaleas.

The dog sniffed the air and shook her massive head. Casually, she trotted past the birdbath, sat with her back to the azaleas, and yawned. "I see you," she said over her shoulder.

Buddy stayed where he was. Seconds became hours. Minutes, years.

"Incidentally, I can also smell you," the dog continued, flopping onto her side. "You might as well come out."

Raising his head, Buddy evaluated the best escape route, which was iffy at best. "So we both see each other. Now what?"

The shepherd rolled to her back, twisting her head toward the bushes and staring through the glossy leaves. "Now you come out and tell me what you're doing in my yard."

"Don't do it!" Orie screeched from behind a caladium. "Run! Run!"

Buddy assessed the situation. Instinct told him this wasn't a cat killer or she would have attacked him by now, but you could never be too careful. Taking a deep breath, he moved warily from his position, eyes fixed on the dog still watching from her upside-down position. "Sorry about the trespassing thing." He tried to appear calm, but every nerve flashed danger.

"There've been some problems, and I'm just passing through. I won't stay long . . . just hungry and . . ." his voice cracked "sort of . . . thirsty."

Twisting from side to side, the dog scratched her back on the dewy grass, groaning with pleasure. "What kind of problems?"

"Some friends of mine are . . . they're lost."

"White cat and a calico?"

Buddy started forward, then stopped himself. "You've seen them?"

"Yesterday." Resting huge paws on her chest, she snapped at a butterfly. "They went off with another cat. Big. Gray." Rolling to her side she curled her lip, exposing scissor-sharp teeth. "And rude. I don't mind cats. What I hate is rude." She lurched to her feet, and Buddy tensed, ready to run.

"Come on, there's some food left from last night, and there's always water over there."

"Are you crazy?" Orie had crawled through the O'Connells' fence and now clung to the chain-link in panic. "Get out!"

Buddy paused. Normally he would never believe a dog. He realized Indoors were forced to cohabit with many undesirables, but Ferals never trusted canines. Never. It was The Law.

Silently the shepherd waited as though aware of Buddy's struggle. There was something about the dog, a feeling of trust Buddy had never experienced with another species. Not fully understanding why, he walked to her side. "Thanks for the offer."

At first he tried to drink with one eye scanning for danger, but thirst overcame him. He greedily gulped the cool liquid, licking the bowl long after it was empty.

The German shepherd sat in the shade of a redbud, listlessly scratching one ear. "My name's Tenba."

"I'm Buddy. I live with The Boy over there." He indicated the house, then sniffed. "Food?"

Tenba motioned toward the porch, and Buddy eagerly raced to the pan, grabbing large dry chunks and swallowing them whole.

"Thanks, that was good." Sinking into the grass, Buddy felt tired and completely overwhelmed by the task before him. "Could you tell me which way they went?"

"I can do better than that." Tenba rose to her feet with arthritic care, took a few hobbling steps, and stretched. "I'll trail them for you."

"Do you want to die?" Orie screamed from under a caladium. "Because I don't think it's considered a 'good deed' if you die!"

Ignoring him, Buddy surveyed the sturdy enclosure. "Thanks for the offer, but it looks like you're locked in here pretty tight."

Tenba shook her head. "Don't let my limp fool you. Once I get warmed up, I can still leave here whenever I want." Legs slightly splayed but with a strong gait, she loped to the rear of the yard and gracefully sailed over the fence and into the alley. Then she jumped back into the yard and stopped, legs wobbling only slightly. "No problem."

A feeble but relentless scratching came from the underbrush where Orie lay entangled in a morning glory vine. With delicate tendrils wound around one hind foot, the lizard frantically inched back toward the O'Connells' side of the fence.

Tenba galloped toward the noise and pushed her graying muzzle close. "I know this one," she said with disgust. "Cranky, mean, and curses a lot. Hey!" she shouted in the lizard's ear. "You've got a dirty mouth!"

Orie jumped, stared at the giant nose, and shut his eyes. "I am special! I was saved for great things," he chanted.

"What's it doing?" Tenba asked.

"I'm not really sure, but his name is Orie," Buddy said, jumping between the dog and his friend. "He's a little different, but okay . . . in a hateful sort of way."

His eyes tightly shut, the reptile lay in a Zen-like trance, repeating the mantra with increasing volume. "I am special! I was saved—"

Buddy batted the mottled head with a gentle paw. "You're fine, Orie, relax. This is Tenba. She's going to help me find my friends."

The lizard opened one eye, now inches from the shepherd's panting jaws. "That's nice," he said, squeezing his eye closed again.

Snapping the vine with his teeth, Buddy carefully pushed him through the chain-link and into the O'Connells' yard. "I think you should go back under the house and get some rest," he said softly. "Go on now, you've been a real friend, and I won't forget you."

Orie lay like a stone.

Buddy reached through the chain, nudging him again.

"Listen to me," Buddy said, enunciating carefully as

though speaking to a child. "Time . . . to . . . go . . . under . . . the . . . house." Slowly, the lizard got to his feet, his face dazed and dreamy. "Yes, I think I will rest now," he mumbled, tottering toward the vent. With a beatific smile and a feeble little wave, he fell into the crawl space, a tendril of the morning glory trailing behind him.

The two animals moved slowly, occasionally stopping as the shepherd sniffed a leaf or bush. For the first six blocks they stuck close to the houses and foliage, but once they passed out of their neighborhood, they used the sidewalk. Tenba trotted briskly along the curb, eyes alert, tail up.

Then abruptly, she stopped, snorting with irritation. "Arrogant, really arrogant. This guy wants to be followed. He's left a trail a chicken could track."

Buddy said nothing. He, too, smelled Jett's pungent scent.

"This is so easy it's not even any fun," Tenba grumbled. "Give me a dismembered corpse, frozen stiff, and stuffed in a sewer. Now that separates purebreds from mutts."

With a frustrated huff, they crossed into the next block and turned into an alley where Tenba spent the next hour tracking between fence lines and dumpsters. "Looks like they're headed toward the highway," she said, panting.

Her breath seemed strained and labored, and Buddy wondered if arthritis was her only problem. "Why don't we take a break?" he said. "There's some shade beneath that jasmine, and I could use a breather."

"Sounds good." Tenba wheezed, joining him beneath the glossy snarl of vines. "I'll stay with you for a little while longer." Squinting at the sun directly above them, the big dog stretched on her side. "Then I have to get back before my woman realizes I'm gone."

Buddy stared down the alley and felt a flash of familiarity. Shaking it away, he nodded at the dog. "Leave whenever you need to; I'm just grateful you came this far."

"It's been interesting." Tenba gave a phlegmy cough, chest heaving with effort. "Sorry I've had to stop so much, but it's just too hot. I haven't tracked anything in a long time . . . out of shape."

"I'm a little soft myself," Buddy said, scratching his ear and suddenly realizing fleas were part of his life again. "I've been wondering . . . I mean, why *are* you helping me like this?"

"Don't really know. Bored, maybe. I haven't done this since I retired from the search-and-rescue team, and besides" her eyes narrowed "Jett's become a real nuisance."

Buddy stiffened. "You know him?"

"Sure, we all know Jett around here. Showed up about a month ago, been hanging around, disturbing some younger dogs in the neighborhood, fighting with the local cats. You know the type." Raising her head, she looked squarely at the tom. "But I don't have to tell you about him, do I? I have a feeling you know him well."

The two animals looked for a long moment into one another's eyes.

"Yes," Buddy said quietly. "He's my brother."

NINE

SUN SHONE ON THE DINING ROOM TABLE, and Shan Dara stretched her long, taupe body against its gleaming surface and yawned. Ceiling fans whirred through the house, and the warm mahogany felt good on her belly despite the oppressive heat of the day. Squirming into a more comfortable position, her periwinkle eyes began to close . . . then suddenly opened wide.

Two forms glided across the street.

Raising her head, she squinted against the glare.

A lanky yellow tom slunk among the bushes, and behind him, nose to the ground, was a German shepherd.

Could the cat be in danger? Shan Dara looked closer. The dog didn't seem aggressive; in fact, it appeared they were together in some way. There was something familiar about the feline, but what? An image floated in her mind; golden eyes, subtle tabby stripes on flaxen fur and something else; a warm, heady feeling she couldn't articulate. Suddenly, she remembered! The tom at the veterinarian's office! His name was . . . what? Her tail twitched with frustration, the answer blocked. Leaping to the floor, she crept to the picture window, watching with fascination as the unlikely duo continued on their way.

"What are you doing?"

The Siamese jumped at the question, feeling strangely violated. "Frank! Stop creeping up on me! I'm just standing here."

"No you're not." The Dachshund moved closer, muscular body alert. "You're looking at something, what is it?"

"Nothing." She groomed her shoulder with forced disinterest. "Go away."

Strutting to the window, Frank jammed his pointed nose against the pane.

Across the street, the German shepherd rolled in the grass, while the cat stood in the shadows scratching his ear.

The hair on the little dog's back bristled, and his tail was straight and still. "A female," he mumbled.

"Frank," Shan Dara said, "you know what happened last time. The stitches? The blood?"

"I love German shepherds."

"But they're too big!" she wailed.

"I love them big," Frank said, beginning to pant. "And more importantly—" he pawed the floor like a bull—"they love me!" With a lusty yelp, he shot into the kitchen, stubby legs scrambling on the linoleum, and hurled toward the screen door like a rocket. His compact body hit the panel with a thump, and the wires pushed outward. Eyes glittering, he prepared for a second try. "I can't help myself. Those big,

Teutonic types just kill me!" He slammed the sagging screen once more. This time a small corner pulled away from the wooden frame. With a grunt, he clamped his teeth around the wire, pulling with a frenzied strength that belied his size.

Bowing in the opposite direction, the frame suddenly separated from the door, and Frank sailed across the linoleum, crashing into the stove.

Jumping to his feet he stared at the ragged hole. "Hang on, Fräulein, here comes Daddy!" With a burst of speed he streaked through the opening and almost cleared the steps before a large hand snagged his hind leg, yanking him back into the kitchen.

"Frank, you get in here right now, you bad dog! Bad, bad dog! Connie! Frank just tried to get outside again!"

A rolled-up newspaper thwacked the Dachshund's pointed nose, and the little dog twisted onto his back, paws tucked against his ribs in submission, silky ears framing either side of his head like a fan.

The man was unmoved. "You are a bad dog!" he shouted again, bringing the paper down against the animal's shiny flank.

Instantly, Frank's demeanor changed. Springing from his supine position, he lunged at the newspaper and, with a carefully aimed snap, shredded not only the headlines but his owner's thumb as well.

"Ouch! Why, you little . . . Connie! He bit me!" The big hand grabbed the dog by the collar, dragging him across the glossy floor. "That's it. I'm locking him in the bedroom!"

Frank's choking snarls of protest faded into the distance. "Ow! Damn it! He bit me again!"

A door slammed.

An odd silence descended.

Shan Dara crept from beneath the dining room table and scurried to the kitchen where tiny bits of newspaper lay scattered on the floor.

With practiced daintiness, she stepped over the debris, paused briefly at the ruined door, then slipped through the ragged edges into the smoldering afternoon.

Shan Dara had never been outside before, and the concrete kitchen steps felt rough and hot on her paws. Shadows danced on the sidewalks as elm saplings bent and waved in the breeze. She slunk toward the front of the house and almost to the porch, just as a lawn mover roared from a neighboring yard. Terrified, she darted behind a hibiscus, crouching beneath its vermilion blooms, her sides heaving with panic.

Across the street Buddy and the dog seemed unconcerned and stopped beneath an oak tree.

Tilting her head, Shan Dara sniffed the humid air. Dark clouds gathered to the east, but the sun still beat in fiery waves against her back, and she longed for shade. Inhaling deeply, she gave a silent thanks to Mother and nodded with satisfaction. It was definitely the tom; his scent was strong and unmistakable. Creeping into a flower bed, Shan Dara settled beneath a cluster of wilting gardenias, prepared to wait.

TEN

THE HUMIDITY OF AN IMPENDING STORM wrapped the shed in heat. Unlike the other three cats, Soot hadn't slept. Instead he sat quietly outside the structure, staring at the house next door.

It was small and dirty, with buckled siding and a hail-damaged roof. Brown grass poked up through clumps of dirt, with only weeds adding greenery to the scraggly landscape. It wasn't the house that interested him, however, but the old woman who lived there. He'd first seen her sitting by the window, one frail, blue-veined hand holding a cup, the other clutching the neck of her gown. Fascinated, Soot crept closer, watching throughout the night as her small frame shuffled from room to room.

Sometimes the old woman moved with purpose, rinsing dishes or folding clothes, but mostly she sat in the dark, massaging her knee and listening to a radio. Around dawn, she pulled on a tattered blue robe, made a sandwich, and limped onto the porch.

That's when she saw him.

"Well, look at you." Carefully, she lowered herself into

the rocker, patted her thigh, and made a little whistling noise.
"Come on. Come on over here, you skinny little thing."

Alarmed, Soot darted beneath a bush, but he was
amazed. She hadn't yelled, thrown rocks, or done any of the
things he associated with humans. He felt a powerful urge to
walk up on the porch and lay by her feet.

She called again, this time putting a small bit of sandwich by her foot and inching it toward him with her toe.

Soot responded with a shy meow, and she chortled with
delight.

"You smell that tuna, don't ya?"

They continued this way for some time; the old woman
rocking and talking, and Soot hunkered in the shadows,
frightened she might approach him and equally afraid she
wouldn't.

Finally the old woman stood, placed the rest of her sandwich on the top step of the porch, and hobbled inside.

Soot panicked, fearing she wouldn't come back, but his
stomach ached from hunger, and the smell of fish overrode
his anxiety. Darting to the steps, he consumed the food in
three bites. It was too rich for his empty stomach, and suddenly nauseated, he vomited on the steps. Thoughts that the
other cats might be awake and ready to leave seemed unim-
portant. He sat motionless beneath the overcast sky, eyes focused
on the screen door, mosquitoes buzzing around his head.

Unbelievably, the old woman reappeared, this time with
a bowl of milk. "Look what I've got, Blackie," she crooned,
placing it in the same spot as before. "Poor little crooked-
tailed boy. Granny's got you some breakfast."

With a squeak of relief, Soot jumped to his feet, then stopped. He had misjudged humans before.

"Nobody's gonna hurt you," the old woman said as though reading his mind.

He meowed softly, moving an inch closer.

"Yes you are, you're just a skinny little thing." She sank into the rocker and patted her lap. "Come on up here to Granny."

Memories of the alley, its bitter winter winds and parched summer days, swept through Soot's brain. How many nights had he skulked through neighborhoods, watching from shadows as Indoors lounged plump and serene behind brightly lit windows? A lifetime of longing gripped his heart, and he crept up the first step.

"Come on, come on," she encouraged, leaning forward, hand extended.

He moved onto the second step, head craning toward her fingertips, and was almost to the third, when a crack of thunder boomed from above. Startled, Soot scrambled to the ground, bolting through the weeds and brambles to the safety of the shed next door. He sat in despair, eyes focused on the porch . . . and empty rocker.

"What do you suppose that delicious smell could be?" A smooth voice drifted from the shadows.

Soot turned with a start. "I—I don't know," he stammered.

A stab of lightning flashed, illuminating Jett as he slunk from the darkness. "Oh, but surely you smell it, too."

Thunder exploded again, and Soot jumped and cringed.

"Could it be some kind of fish?" Jett continued, tilting his huge head toward the black cat's face and sniffing. "Tuna, perhaps?"

Soot backed away. "No—I mean, yes. I found some food . . . over . . . there." His voice trailed off as he looked toward the old woman's house.

Jett gazed at the threatening sky, sniffing the thick, wet air with distaste. "You say you found it over there?" Casually, he inspected his tail.

Soot nodded, as a giant paw caught him behind the ear.

"And you *ate* it?" Jett roared, pinning him to the ground. "You took food offered by a human and *ate* it?"

Soot screeched with fear.

Pris and Zekki started to their feet, staggering to the door of the shed.

"What's wrong?" Zekki shouted. "What's happening?"

Eye bright with fury, Jett swiveled his head to the right. "He's broken The Law of the Feral! Never trust humans! Never be touched by humans!" Releasing Soot, who scurried away, he stared at Pris. "You would never make *that* mistake, would you?" He growled. "You would never do anything *that* stupid?"

Terrified, Pris cringed into the shadows.

Zekki pushed forward. "But he was probably just hungry, sir. We haven't eaten in a long time, and human food is good. It's—it's . . . we eat it every day, sir."

"Every day," Pris repeated.

"Not anymore," Jett hissed. "You're in the Outs now, my dear, and things have changed."

Lightning jagged through boiling clouds, and a drop of rain splattered in the dust.

"This is what you wanted, isn't it?" Jett crept toward the cats with serpentlike stealth. "To be out at last, free and feral?"

A crack of thunder belched from the heavens.

"Well, you got your wish," he whispered. "Now obey The Law!" Rain pelted his eyeless socket, streaming down his face in darkening rivulets. "Get inside the garage and stay there until I come back. You'll eat *what* I tell you and *when* I tell you."

Abruptly he turned, disappearing behind the torrent of water that now poured from the sky.

Zekki and Pris scrambled into the shed, huddling beneath a wheelbarrow for comfort. Soot staggered behind, a thin smear of blood streaking his neck. With effort, he clamored to the ledge of a small window overlooking the old woman's house.

Another streak of lightning illuminated the landscape, and he started, staring through the dingy glass at the scene below.

Jett strode through the old woman's yard, water dripping from his thick coat and gathering on his whiskers. Reaching the porch, he glided up the steps and walked deliberately to where the bowl of milk still sat. He began to drink.

Wind blew gusts of rain onto the deck, and the old woman stood behind the screen door stamping her feet and clapping her hands in a feeble attempt to chase him away.

Ignoring her, Jett continued his meal, as Soot watched, incredulous, stomach churning with hunger.

Finishing the last of the milk, Jett licked his whiskers, then glared at the shed window. In one easy motion he turned his back on Soot, gave a comfortable stretch, and proceeded to spray the empty bowl with a hard stream of urine.

• • •

Rain peppered the tin roof like bullets, and Pris and Zekki

crept from their hiding place.

"I'm hungry," Pris whimpered, "and thirsty."

"Me too," Zekki said.

"What if Jett never comes back and just leaves us here to starve?" Pris's voice shook. "We don't know where we are or how to get back, and he was . . . so mean." Ducking her head, she started to cry.

Zekki shifted from one paw to the other. "Everything's all right. He probably just acted that way to make us understand The Law so we'd be safe." Something flickered at the back of his mind. What had Buddy said about The Law? Hunger clouded his memory, and he shook his head in confusion. "Look," he said, trying to appear confident despite the dread knotting his gut. "Jett promised we'd get out of here tonight, and I'm sure we'll eat something then." Scanning the murky interior for Soot, Zekki finally saw the black cat hunched in the shadows. "Won't we, Soot? He wouldn't let us starve, would he? I mean, even Jett has to eat sometime, right?"

"Yes," Soot's voice drifted quietly from the darkness. "Even Jett has to eat . . . sometime."

ELEVEN

TENBA STOOD IN THE GRASS, face upturned to the swirling rain. Shaking herself, she turned to Buddy who crouched in a miserable clump beneath the oak tree.

"The woman should be home about now, so . . . much as I hate to, I need to go." Water glistened in tiny droplets on her thick coat, and the dog shook again. "She doesn't know I can get out, and it might be sort of a shock. Frankly"—her huge paw carefully rubbed a cloudy eye—"I've got these darn cataracts and can't see too great when it gets dark."

The yellow cat nodded, but his demeanor seemed distant and sad.

Flattening her ears against the steady downpour, the dog watched him closely. "You're worrying about The Boy, aren't you?"

Buddy blinked and suddenly felt like crying. "Yes."

"Don't," she said. "He'll be fine."

"But he depends on me. I don't know what he'll do without me."

"Why?" her voice was calm and even. "Is he stupid?"

"Absolutely not!" Buddy felt a rush of anger. "He's extremely smart, does great in school, has lots of friends—"

"Then maybe," she said gently, "you're the one that's afraid to be without *him*."

Buddy stood motionless, rain trailing down his shoulders and puddling around his paws. Could it be true? Was he afraid? He had to admit there'd never been danger or responsibility on Sixth Avenue, only safety, acceptance, and love. And now that was all gone, and he was back where he had started. "It's hard to leave. He saved my life."

"And after his father left, you saved his." Tenba blinked, dim eyes wise and kind. "But ultimately, we all walk alone, and there are many paths to Sho-valla."

A hum of thunder rolled in the distance, and the rain slowed to a drizzle.

Her words were soothing, and though still confused, the cat felt a momentary sense of peace. "I guess I'd never thought about it like that."

"I have the feeling there are lots of things you haven't thought about." The shepherd cocked her head.

Buddy frowned. "What do you mean?"

"Well, for instance, The Cat Master."

"I don't understand."

"He's dead." Tenba gave the yellow tom a penetrating look. "What do you think about that?"

The ground seemed to slant beneath his paws, and Buddy fought for equilibrium. "Dead?" he finally managed to murmur. "When?"

The shepherd groaned and stretched her back legs. "Couple of nights ago. There's been lots of mind-talk going on right now. Sometimes I eavesdrop a little." She casually licked a puddle. "Wonder who the old cat chose as his successor?"

Rise from the alley . . . rise from the alley . . .

Snippets from the dream drifted back, and Buddy shook them away. He felt strangely off balance and muddled. "I—I don't know. Do you?"

"No. There was some type of disturbance that blurred the connection . . . something very unfriendly. Mind-talk is delicate. It can't handle dark thoughts." Tenba watched the cat's face carefully. "Are you sure you didn't hear anything?"

Buddy's heart banged like a timpani. "No. But . . . I mean, thanks for telling me."

"Glad to help." The old shepherd sniffed the air. "Unfortunately, the rain is going to wash most of their scents away."

"It doesn't matter," Buddy said, glad the subject had changed. "Mother will help me."

"Have any idea where they are?"

An unexpected vision of trees, water, and lush greens jolted his mind. It felt both familiar and frightening, and he furrowed his brow, perplexed. "Not exactly where they *are*, but maybe . . . where they're *going*."

The dog moved closer, graying head inches from Buddy's face. "Just make sure you know where *you're* going." With a last shake, she trotted down the street, turned a corner, and was gone.

Buddy drew a shaky breath and sank to his haunches.

The Cat Master was dead! He'd always heard Indoors were telepathically impaired, but he was a Feral and had been proficient at mind-talk since kittenhood. Why hadn't he heard the news along with everyone else, and more importantly, why hadn't Jett mentioned it? Wariness prickled the hairs along his spine. Tenba said that the connection had been broken. She'd been right. Only the darkest of thoughts could have interfered with The Cat Master's powers of communication. Who would have done that, and why? Fatigue numbed his mind, and he sighed. He'd think about this later, when he wasn't so tired. Rising to his feet, he cut through a yard and onto a side street.

Dying gardens shimmered beneath a sprinkle of dew, and the last scents of summer filled his nose. Hopping a puddle, he moved toward the alley, its muddy gloom a harsh contrast to the bright, manicured neighborhood.

He'd only traveled a few blocks before the stench of urine and feces became strong. A kaleidoscope of memories rushed back with breathtaking force.

Two kittens pranced in the sun, one yellow, the other gray. Tumbling in the dust, they scampered in circles, pouncing and bristling in mock battle, eventually collapsing together in a loving heap.

Lost in the vision, Buddy was startled by the sound of rustling behind him. Instinctively he whirled, fangs bared, ears flat.

Periwinkle eyes stared at him with surprise. "I didn't mean to scare you."

Disoriented, the tom blinked hard, trying to separate the past from the present.

"It's me," she persisted. "Shan Dara. We met at the vet's."

Buddy recoiled in shock. "Shan Dara?" he said, suddenly aware that he was wet, rumpled, and probably smelled of dog.

"I saw you outside my window." She nodded toward the street. "I live over there."

Buddy managed a loopy smile. "Well, ho . . . hoo . . . I mean, howdy," he finally blurted, wondering where he had come up with such a ridiculous greeting.

The Siamese seemed not to notice and gently bumped his neck in a shy greeting.

Her touch burned like a brand.

"I hope I'm not bothering you or anything. I saw you and wanted to say, uh . . . howdy." She made an odd little gesture with her head. "It's wonderful to see you again, Bubba."

Buddy stared in wonderment. She was here! She was real! She remembered his name! No, wait a minute, that wasn't his name. "My name's Buddy," he said.

"Oh, I'm sorry! Of course, it's Buddy."

He winced at her embarrassment. How rude. How insensitive. He should have changed his name. "That's okay; you can call me anything."

Drops of water spattered from the bushes, and a trio of sparrows quarreled from a fence.

The cats stood awkwardly gazing at one another.

Buddy cleared his throat. "I—I guess you probably want to get back home now. I mean I've got to go, and I want to see you safely inside before I leave."

Shan Dara licked a perfect taupe paw and lowered her eyes. "I don't really want to go home right now. I mean, I've been sitting across the street waiting for the rain to stop so I could talk to you."

There was a strained silence.

"I'm not sure what you're doing out here." She raised her head and took a deep breath. "But I thought whatever it is, maybe we could do it together."

"Together?" A flea popped onto Buddy's leg, and he prayed she hadn't noticed. "But, you don't even know me, and it's dangerous out here." He moved closer. "I'm looking for some friends, the weather is bad, there's dirt and mud, and you're so . . . you're all . . . clean." He tried not to drown in the intensity of her eyes. "I don't understand."

The Siamese moved closer, touching his nose with hers. "I can't explain it. I just know that I've thought about you a lot since we met, and I get so tired of just watching things happen through the window. I won't be any trouble. Can't I come with you?"

Buddy found it hard to concentrate. Her fur smelled of flowers, and her blue eyes obliterated the clouds.

"Can I . . . come with you?" she repeated.

Buddy jolted himself to the present. The answer, of course, was no, absolutely not. There were things to do, dangerous things, and a companion would only slow him down. "Yes," he said, "I'd like that."

Side by side they walked deeper into the alley. Thunder still rolled in the distance, but a rainbow arced across the horizon, streaking the sky with trails of pastels.

• • •

Mud was everywhere, seeping through puddles and sticking like paste to their fur and paws.

Buddy walked in front, carefully picking out the paths least difficult to maneuver, and Shan Dara followed, creamy belly splattered with water and debris. The afternoon light was dimming, and the area grew more hostile as they moved further down the block.

"Wouldn't it be easier to walk on the sidewalk?" Shan Dara finally asked, stopping to lick a glob of muck from her chest.

"I'm really sorry about all this," Buddy said, ears cocked forward. "But it's safer if you just follow me."

A cloudy twilight hampered their vision, and though things seemed quiet, Buddy had the prickly sensation they weren't alone.

Something rumbled through the alley, and they darted inside a crate, eyes reflecting like neon orbs in the truck's headlights.

"I don't like this place." Shan Dara flicked a dirty paw with irritation. "It's so—so filthy."

"It sure is," Buddy said a little too loudly. "Disgusting."

Creeping into the open, Shan Dara looked around, mouth pursed with distaste. "Can you believe some animals actually live here?"

"No," Buddy mumbled, heart hammering with an uncontrollable fear. "I—I can't."

Sighing, Shan Dara shook her head. "Everything is so ugly, and there's no place to sleep or eat or—"

"That was a lie," he interrupted, staring at the ground. "I just lied to you."

The Siamese frowned with confusion. "A lie?"

"I acted like I've never been in an alley before, but that's a lie." Buddy swallowed hard. "I've been here plenty of times."

"You have?"

"I was born here, it's my home." The words stuck in his throat like sand. He coughed and looked away.

"But that's not possible." Shan Dara's blue eyes widened. "You're not feral. You live in a house with a nice family like I do." Suddenly, she laughed, batting his head with a playful paw. "Oh, you're just kidding around! This is a joke, right?"

Her touch grazed his ear like a kiss, and he pulled away before he was tempted to lie again. "No, it's not a joke. I'm a Feral whether I look like it or not. I lived with The Boy for a while, but—but this is where I was born."

"You can't be," she protested. "Feral cats are . . . well, they're sick and dirty and mean."

He gazed at her patrician face, perfected through centuries of care and breeding, and thought of his mother, siblings, and friends. He remembered their lives in the alley—the price paid for those lives—and felt a surge of anger mixed with pride. "I think you should go home now."

"But that's not fair, all I said was—"

"I know," he interrupted. "You said Ferals were sick, dirty, and mean, and sometimes that's true. But they're also tough and brave and lots of other things an Indoor could never understand." He looked away, heart heavy with a dream turned to dust. "I don't expect you to understand . . . I just . . . this isn't going to work."

Shan Dara's eyes looked hurt. "But I—I didn't know. How could I know?"

"You couldn't. I'm the one who lied, not you." Mortified, he faced her. "Ferals and Indoors are forbidden to mix anyway. It's The Law."

She stood silently, her graceful form backlit by a hazy moon, and Buddy wondered if he'd ever seen anything so beautiful or so terribly out of place. "It's not your fault. None of this is your fault. I'm sorry." He met her frightened gaze. "Don't worry; I'll see that you get home."

There was a thump from the shadows, and both cats jumped with surprise.

A lumpy form ambled from behind a trash can. It lurched and stumbled, then finally stopped. "Water," it said.

Buddy quickly stepped in front of the Siamese, tail bristled. "Who are you?"

The creature staggered closer, a streetlight illuminating its face.

"Oh, it's only a raccoon," Shan Dara said, obviously relieved. "I was afraid it was a dog or something."

Eyeing her dully, the stranger tried to swallow and gagged. "Water," it croaked louder.

"Water?" she repeated. "But it's been raining all day,

and there's water everywhere."

Something sinister squirmed in Buddy's brain. "We don't have any water," he said evenly. "Maybe there's some in the next block."

The coon's demeanor changed. Rage contorted its features, and it snapped the air in fury. "Raining? Raining?" It lurched forward.

Buddy hissed, paw raised in warning, and the animal stopped, rocking in agitation.

"Water's bad, water's bad!" it chanted. The large head bobbed and swayed, ropy saliva dripping from its jaws.

"He's rabid," Buddy whispered.

"Rabidy babidy, bad." It drooled, gazing with sudden fascination at the sky.

"Shan Dara, there's a chinaberry tree behind us." Buddy's voice was steady and calm. "Back up really slowly."

"I—I can't—I—"

"Listen, just listen. When I tell you, run to the tree . . . climb it fast!"

Shan Dara moved one step.

Snapping to attention, the coon refocused, his eyes bright with insanity.

"Easy, easy . . . ," Buddy said. "As soon as you move, I'll try to divert him."

The creature clicked its teeth and took a lurching step.

"Now! Do it now!"

Shan Dara vaulted up the slender trunk, and Buddy pushed forward, slashing the coon's black muzzle with a well-aimed claw.

Undaunted, it jumped past him onto the slippery bark.

"Faster! Faster! Just keep going!" Buddy sprang onto the tree, desperately trying to overtake them.

Furiously, the raccoon snapped at the Siamese's retreating form, blood and saliva spraying her flank, clinging in foamy globules to her fur.

"Go! Don't look back!" Buddy's fangs barely missed the ringed tail dangling inches above. He could see Shan Dara had almost reached the uppermost branch, but the coon was still clamoring behind, and the fragile tree bent and swayed with their weight.

"What the heck's going on back here!" a man's voice boomed.

Footsteps squished in the mud, and a powerful beam of light shone on the trio.

For an instant the raccoon froze, masked face blank with confusion. Buddy shinnied up past him, joining Shan Dara on an upper bough, where they both clung in terror.

Dripping saliva, the creature watched with interest as the man poked an overturned garbage can with the toe of his boot.

A little boy trailed behind, eyes wide, watching from the shadows.

"Well, now, lookie here, Jamie," the man hooted, shining a flashlight first on the boy, then into the tree. "We got a big ol' coon that's treed a couple of cats."

The raccoon hissed and snapped at a leaf.

"So you're the little creeps that've been tearin' up my

garbage and making a mess back here." The man handed the flashlight to the boy and eased a shotgun to his shoulder. "You know what I think?" he drawled, drawing a bead on the cats and then the raccoon. "I think there's about to be three less vermin in the world."

Squinting into the gun site, he slowly pulled the trigger.

TWELVE

ZEKKI PACED IN THE DUST. His white coat was matted with debris and hung in gray, twisted strands from his body. It had been dark for some time, and still there was no sign of Jett. "If he's not back soon, I think we should leave," Zekki said with a confidence he didn't feel.

Pris peeked from behind a bag of potting soil. "And go home?"

"Definitely, we'll just go home."

"Is that right?" Jett stood motionless in the shed's doorway, the moon casting an eerie glow on his eye. Raising one paw, he carefully licked a callused pad. "And just where is home?" With a dramatic twist of his head, he quickly looked to the right. "Would it be that way?" He swiveled his head to the left. "Or could it be this way?" Lowering himself to his belly, he peered beneath a wheelbarrow where Zekki had scurried in terror. "What would you guess, my interfering friend? Left, right, up, down? Be careful, though. Your pals are counting on you."

"I—I don't know," Zekki stammered. "I was just, you

know, talking because you've been gone a long time and . . ."
He stopped, clearing his throat.

Mosquitoes buzzed in the damp air, and a dog yipped in
the distance.

"It doesn't matter how long I go away," Jett continued,
his voice steely with anger. "You stay where I tell you to."

Zekki gave a miserable nod, and the big tom suddenly
brightened. "So, how about a head count?" He sent the white
cat a withering glance. "We've established that our big-mouthed
'hero' is hiding beneath a farm implement . . . now, where is our
little calico friend?"

Pris slunk from her hiding place.

"That makes two." Jett peered into the garage. "And Soot?
I'll bet he's all rested and raring to go by now."

Soot clamored from the window ledge, legs shaky from
hunger, eyes dull. Leaning against the wall for support, he
dipped his head.

Jett watched with cold amusement. "Yes, nice and rested.
Let's go." With a flick of his tail, he trotted into the sultry night,
the three young cats straggling behind.

Soot glanced one last time at the old woman's house as they
passed. The porch light was on, but the rest of the structure sat
in darkness. Closing his heart against the bright and friendly
future that had dangled so briefly before him, he staggered after
Pris's fading form . . . and into the gloom of reality.

The alley wound through the neighborhood, finally dead-
ending at a tree-lined boulevard. Traffic was heavy here, and
the animals kept to the shadows, creeping through carefully
trimmed hedges and sprawling hydrangeas laden with fluffy

pink blooms. Eventually the area became more commercial, with small businesses and fast-food restaurants crowding against prefab offices.

The cats pressed on, avoiding human contact, slinking behind gas stations and shriveled landscaping, until they crossed another alley that turned into a parking lot sur-rounded by a theater complex and grocery store.

Jett led them to a dumpster in back of the buildings. "There's food in there. If you want to eat, do it now and do it fast." Scowling, the big cat disappeared beneath a loading dock.

Pris paced in confusion. "But I don't see any bowls. Where's the food?"

"I think it's in that thing." Zekki slowly approached the dumpster, wincing at the pungent smell of rotting produce.

"Don't go inside," Soot said quickly. "Look for food lying around on the ground. Sometimes people throw things in, and they miss. It's dangerous to go in it. You might not be able to get out." He sat heavily. "If you find anything, let me know. I'm just going to rest here for a minute."

Pris timidly approached the black cat and pushed against his neck. "Are you okay?"

"I'm fine. I'm . . . just really tired. Let me know if you find anything, and I'll come over." He tried to purr, but his throat was parched and tight.

She nodded and joined Zekki who was gnawing at a white paper bag.

"Hey, here's something!" he shouted. "It's meat and bread and some other stuff!"

The two cats pulled the hamburger onto the pavement and tore at the remains.

Pushing himself to his feet, Soot crawled toward the food, eyes scanning for hidden threats. "Don't eat it here." Even the dim lighting behind the store was risky, and he was aware of Jett watching from the darkness, waiting for them to be careless. "It's too bright here. Pull it over behind those bushes."

Zekki obliged, and he and Pris devoured the sack's contents, pushing one another out of the way for better leverage.

A soft chuckle floated from beneath the loading dock. "You're wasting your breath. They don't understand and never will." Jett crawled into the open, dropping a dead cricket onto the pavement. "But not you and me, eh, Soot? We understand everything, don't we?" Nodding toward the insect, his eye glittered like polished brass. "No hard feelings about earlier. Consider this a gift from an old friend."

Soot said nothing as he pounced on the creature, crunching it hungrily and wishing there were more.

A soft wind blew from the east, and the sounds of voices echoed in the distance.

Jett's head shot up, and his broad nose probed the air. "Go! Now!" he roared.

Zekki and Pris stood by their meal, bewildered.

"Leave the food! Run!" Soot shouted, adrenalin overcoming his fatigue.

From behind the mall, a procession of boys on bicycles descended into the parking lot. Whooping with laughter, they pumped furiously in between parked cars, heading toward the back of the grocery store.

The cats scattered in panic. Zekki darted beneath the dumpster, while Jett, Soot, and Pris headed for the alley.

"Hey, there're some cats or something back here!" one of the boys yelled. "Corey, throw me your rope. I'm gonna catch one!"

The three cats ran blindly through shrubbery, around trash cans, and over boxes and broken glass.

"Highway, cross the highway!" Jett shouted as he zigzagged through the underbrush.

Bicycles thumped and swooshed behind them, the boys screaming to one another in a frenzy of pursuit.

Soot was failing. His breath came in short, jagged gasps. With a grunt he stumbled, and Pris pushed him to his feet. "Where's Zekki?" she panted, as they regained their stride. "What's happening? Where's the highway?"

"It's straight ahead." Soot wheezed. "Do what Jett says!" He could hear sounds of traffic; the deafening roar of semis and the whiz of cars traveling at high speeds. Suddenly a four-lane blacktop loomed before them, as the boys bore down from behind.

Jett vaulted straight across the first lane. Dodging an oncoming car, he sprinted to the island, where he turned and looked back at Soot and Pris standing on the curb. "Come on!" he bellowed.

Soot pushed Pris from behind. "Go on! Go!"

A wall of traffic appeared in the dusk. Pris took a few tentative steps, then stared at the headlights, paralyzed with fear. In a last burst of energy, Soot jumped into the street, landing hard on the calico's hindquarters. With a squeak she lurched across both lanes and scrambled onto the curb behind Jett.

"I've got him! I've got him!" one of the boys yelled. Skidding to a stop, he hopped from his bike and made a swipe at Soot, who retreated further into the street, hissing with panic.

A horn blared, and the sound of squealing brakes ripped the air.

The boy jumped back, and the cat twisted into the oncoming car.

There was a soft thump as Soot's body bounced off a tire. The impact was painless, and he felt strangely liberated until gravity intervened, slamming him into a crumpled heap against the curb.

The boys clustered in a semicircle, staring with morbid fascination. "Man, did you see that?" one said, slapping the rope against his thigh. "Boom! They popped him good." Squatting for a better look, he prodded the still form with his finger, shrugged, and stood up. "Let's get out of here. I'm hungry." Laughing and swearing, they peddled into the night, raucous voices fading behind them.

Soot lay on the warm pavement, his head twisted to the side, his hind leg turned at an unnatural angle. He could hear the hum of traffic, but it seemed dreamlike and far away.

Someone opened a car door and footsteps crunched in the gravel. "Oh Lord, I hit it! Mother, come over here. I can't look. Is it dead?"

Soot heard another door open and slow, shuffling footsteps approached. There was a sharp intake of breath, then wrinkled hands scooped him from the pavement, cradling him in gentle arms. "Don't you worry, little crooked tail," a familiar voice crooned. "Granny's got you now."

THIRTEEN

THE SHOTGUN BOOMED, and the raccoon jerked off the tree as though yanked by an invisible cord. With a thud, it hit the ground, convulsed, and finally lay quiet, eyes open, still bright with surprise.

Snapping with the release of the animal's weight, the chinaberry gracefully sprang upright, and the cats scrambled to keep their footing.

Swinging the gun higher, the man aimed, pulling the trigger again.

"Jump!" Buddy screamed, as the shot echoed around them. With a grunt he leaped from the tree, arced in midair, and landed on the raccoon's body.

With a squeal the Siamese tumbled behind, twisting through the branches, finally hitting the ground firmly and miraculously on all fours.

With a flurry of mud and leaves, the animals streaked up the alley and over a fence just as a third shot was fired.

"Darn it!" the man roared. "I can't believe it! I can't believe I missed them!"

The boy ran to the raccoon, squatting beside it. "Daddy,

it's got some kind of white stuff all over its face. It's yucky."

Shining the flashlight on the animal, the man yanked the boy back by his collar. "Don't touch it, Jamie! Did you touch it?"

The child shook his head, eyes wide with fear.

A screen door creaked open, and a woman's voice called from the house next door. "Hey, Les, what's going on back there?"

"You're not gonna believe this!" the man shouted back. "But I just shot me a rabid coon over here, and I guarantee there're two cats runnin' around that have it, too. I'm callin' Animal Control first thing in the morning!"

"Mercy!" the woman yelled, shutting the screen with a bang. "That kinda stuff just scares me to death."

The man turned to the boy who had inched his way back to the raccoon's body and was timidly poking it with a stick. "Hey, did you hear what I said?" With a ringing slap to the head, he pulled the child to his feet. "I said for you not to be touchin' it. Let's bag this thing up and put it in the garage."

The boy rubbed his stinging temple and nodded. He liked the garage idea, deciding he'd take a really good look at the coon when his dad was at work. "Okay," he said, following his father into the backyard. "I won't touch it."

The door slammed shut, and the porch light blinked to darkness.

Shan Dara crouched beneath a tangle of trumpet vine. There was a jagged red welt where the pellet had grazed her, and she trembled, eyes dilated and black.

Buddy stood a few feet away, staring into the darkness. "I think we're okay now," he panted. "They don't seem to be coming after us."

"I'm—I'm bleeding." Her voice was weak. "Will I die?"

Trotting to her side, Buddy carefully inspected the wound. "No, it's just a nick. You're going to be fine." He raised his head and warily sniffed the air. "I don't feel safe here, though. We need to keep going and then rest. Can you do that?"

"But I've—I've been hurt!" she cried. "I can't believe something like this could happen! How did this happen?"

Buddy gazed first at her elegant gold collar, now smeared with mud, and then at her bleeding flank. "You're in the Outs now," he said, gently licking the cut. "You may be something else when you're home with your people, but for now . . ." his eyes met hers "you're just another Feral: mean, dirty, diseased . . ."

She winced.

" . . . and brave. You did great back there. I was proud of you."

"You were?"

"Very."

She ducked her head. "I wasn't brave; I was scared out of my mind."

"Courage has nothing to do with bravery. I was scared, too. No one wants to die." He blinked into the darkness. "Not even a raccoon."

Shan Dara moved to his side. "I'm sorry for what I said. Whoever you are, wherever you're from, I'm proud just to be here." She glanced up, and a silvery shaft of moonlight lit her chiseled face. "Do you forgive me?"

"Yes," he said, knowing in that instance he could never begrudge her anything. "I do."

They walked for hours in companionable silence. Bright summer stars illuminated their path as they drifted through shrubbery, nibbling at grasses and drinking from puddles. Occasionally something scuffled in the bushes, and once they saw a Feral scramble beneath a fence, but for the most part, their journey was quiet and uneventful.

Softened by the gentle light of morning, the alley lost much of its dark foreboding. Instead, it stretched for blocks, reduced to weeds and garbage, but still refuge for the many creatures calling it home.

A radio warbled in the distance, and both cats stopped, heads up.

"Wait!" Buddy said, a tickle of excitement bristling the fur along his back. "They've been here!" He sniffed the air. "And not long ago, either. Hide in those weeds and don't move until I get back, okay?"

Shan Dara nodded, sinking smoothly into the foliage.

Jumping a cyclone fence, Buddy crept to the front of a dilapidated shed. The scent was strong, fresh, almost over-powering. Peering inside, he saw a tuft of long white fur beneath a wheelbarrow. Zekki! They couldn't have been gone longer than a couple of hours.

The radio's music seemed louder, and he realized it came from the old house next door. Quickly, Buddy trotted to where Shan Dara waited. "I think we'll be safe in there," he said, indicating the shed. "But be careful, it's getting light, and someone might come out."

Shan Dara scaled the fence, creeping quickly toward the building, then stopped. "You're coming too, right?"

Buddy's eyes locked on hers, calm and unblinking. "I'm not going to leave you."

"I know." She smiled. "I just wanted to hear you say it."

Buddy stood in the pastel morning, relief turning to guilt. The others weren't dead. Mother had preserved their scents, pure and unmistakable. He thought of the young cats, so lost and vulnerable. Why hadn't he foreseen this? They weren't colonized Ferals, hard-wired for survival and possessing innate understanding of their environment. They were Indoors, separated too early from their mothers, put in shelters or pet stores, isolated and ill-prepared for adversity. He remembered their unanswered questions about the Outs; why hadn't he told them more?

Depressed and worried, he walked back to the shed. Shan Dara was already asleep, and he quietly curled up next to her warm body. His muscles throbbed from exhaustion as he drifted into a half state of wakefulness and dream.

Buddy saw himself sitting by a pond, its clear water cool and inviting.

"It's time," a familiar voice whispered from the wetness.

Crouching low, he strained toward the pool. "Ahn-ya! Is that you?"

Her sweet face shimmered up at him from beneath the water, distorting his reflection into a thousand tiny ripples. "Everyone is waiting."

"Waiting for what?" Buddy asked, longing to touch her.

"You know." She stretched her paw toward him, then slipped beneath the foaming waves that suddenly crashed and roiled onto the bank.

Confused, Buddy turned to run, but a dark form loomed behind him, its dripping maw stretched with malevolence, its eye glittering with rage.

Buddy jerked awake, his pulse racing. He suddenly understood! The Cat Master was dead, and Jett was headed to The Gathering.

FOURTEEN

DAWN SPILLED INTO THE PARKING LOT, casting dull light over the few cars still remaining.

Zekki peered from beneath the dumpster. He had spent the night crouched in darkness, terrified to leave its protection and equally afraid of being separated from Pris. With ragged breaths he squirmed into the open. The last thing he remembered before hiding was the boys and Jett's voice telling the cats to run. Now, standing in the friendlier light of day, the night's events held a dreamlike quality that frightened him even more. He had no idea what to do next. His first thought had been to wait here until they all came back for him. But it had been hours now. What if something had happened? The boys sounded mean, and one of them had carried a rope. Zekki blocked the thought from his mind. Jett was too smart to have been caught, but Soot was weak and Pris was . . . his heart wrenched at the thought of her alone with Jett. Pris needed him! He had to find her no matter how afraid he was! But how? Meat and bread were still scattered on the ground, but the thought of food turned his stomach, and he looked away.

"You gonna eat that?" a voice asked.

Terrified, Zekki streaked back under the dumpster.

"Are you?" it persisted. A large gray head thrust its way beneath the metal container, its beady eyes staring with unguarded curiosity.

Zekki shrank as far from the long pointed snout as possible. "What—what are you?"

"Possum," the animal answered amiably. Backing into the open, he shambled to the remains of the hamburger and looked up. "So, are you gonna eat that?"

"What? No." Zekki said.

Gobbling the meat, the creature focused on the bread. "How about this? You gonna eat this?"

"No."

The possum nudged a pickle. "How about this?"

"No! No! Eat the whole thing!" Zekki shouted, scrunching further into the shadows.

The visitor happily obliged, scarfing french fries, lettuce, and finally a portion of the paper bag. Belching with satisfaction, he squatted by the dumpster, waiting.

Moments passed. The sun climbed higher in the sky, beating down on the metal container.

"Are you gonna stay under there long?" the possum finally shouted. "I've been up all night, and that's normally where I sleep!"

Zekki shifted uncomfortably. He was hot and cramped and more than a little tired of his surroundings. Warily, he made his way into the open, crept a safe distance from the animal, and sat down. He wanted to speak, but his throat was dry, and it took several tries. "I'm sort of lost, and maybe you can help me out," he squeaked.

The possum looked blank. "Help you with what?"

"Well," Zekki continued, moving a little closer, "I was here with my friends last night. Some boys came, my friends ran, and . . ." he stopped, not sure what to say next. "And I don't know where they went."

A car swung through the lot, and both animals scurried for cover. Waiting calmly until it was gone, the possum spotted a dead roach and waddled into the sun. He looked up. "Are you gonna—?"

Zekki shook his head.

Slurping it with vigor, the possum coughed and cleared his throat. "Okay, kids come through here all the time. I figure your friends probably headed that way." He nodded toward the alley.

"Yes!" Zekki said, flicking his tail with excitement. "They did!"

"Then they probably ran to the highway and crossed it. That's what I'd do."

"I've heard of highways . . ."

The possum glanced around the parking lot. "They look a lot like this, only thinner. But be careful. Lots of cars and—" He stopped, mesmerized by an ant-covered blob of bubble gum on the pavement, and looked questioningly at the cat.

"No, no, it's yours," Zekki said quickly, fighting a wave

of nausea. "And thanks for the information."

"Okey dokey," the creature muttered, carefully pulling at the pink substance which stretched and finally popped from the asphalt. Sucking it into his mouth, he swallowed. "Good luck."

Zekki ran across the parking lot, turned into the alley, and stopped. The smell of the animals was strong. He knew they had headed west, probably toward the highway as the possum had said, but he was afraid to continue. A dog barked from an adjoining yard. Startled, the young cat charged forward, twisting and turning through the debris until he heard the thunder of engines and wheels.

Creeping toward the curb, he stared at the grimy asphalt. Cars swirled past, the force of their motion whipping the long fur back from his head and chest. Taking a deep breath, he sniffed the air, and Mother rewarded him with a mélange of information. Pris and Soot had been here, but there was another smell: metallic, sweet, and much closer. Looking down, he shrank back in horror. Blood! There was blood on the curb!

A car horn blared, and he turned in panic. Dashing toward the alley, he bolted over a cyclone fence, ran blindly through two yards, and finally darted beneath a rusted car, where he crouched, heart thumping with terror. Raising his head, Zekki uttered a high, keening yowl of desperation. There had been blood, and it was fresh. But whose blood was it and where were the others now?

FIFTEEN

ORIE AWOKE WITH A YELP, sounds of the cat's desolate cry reverberating in his head. Scanning the crawl space, he blinked in bewilderment.

Upstairs, the house was eerily quiet. No thumps, laughter, or cat games disturbed the silence. Even The Boy, whose pacing had finally stopped, seemed nonexistent.

"Bad dream," he said. Or was it? He had definitely been asleep, but the sound wasn't really dreamlike. This was more like telepathic conversation, something he found so boring, he rarely paid attention to it. Could it be he'd tapped into some faraway creatures he'd never heard before? Cows, maybe, or fish? The lizard remembered the screams and shivered. No, it had definitely been a feline cry; loud, desperate, and impossible to ignore. But whose screams were they, and how and why had the cat contacted him? A tickly sensation glided up his spine. "I'm special," he reminded himself quickly. "I was saved for great things."

Orie's voice echoed in the crawl space.

Dust floated in the air.

The feeling remained.

"Something's weird," he said to no one in particular. Slithering through the vent, he pulled himself into the backyard and noted the German shepherd was out and dozing next door.

An ant crawled over the lizard's toe. Tongue flicking, he slurped it with gusto. "Good-bye," he said cheerily, preparing to finish off its friends and family now plodding in dogged determination over his right foot.

Tell the dog, the voice-like feeling pushed.

"What?" Orie spun in panic. This time it wasn't a sound; this time it was totally different. He stopped, cocked his head, and listened.

Foliage rustled in the breeze and a squirrel chattered from the roof.

"I'm just hungry." The thought was comforting, and with renewed interest he focused on the ant procession winding through the grass.

Tell the dog!

Darting beneath a marigold, Orie squinted with fury through the petals. "Leave me alone! I'm not telling the dog! Get some other moron to tell the dog!"

Tell the dog, now! it boomed.

The ants disappeared under some rotting leaves, and Orie raised and lowered his body in a repetitive, hydraulic motion, heart thundering with fear. The voice was gone, but the feeling remained.

That *feeling*.

From next door, the shepherd groaned, flopping onto her side.

The lizard narrowed his eyes. She would go in soon. Perhaps the best thing would be to return to the crawl space, sleep things off, get back to his old self. "I'm special, you know," he snarled defensively.

Hurry, before she goes in!

The directive was so intense that Orie flinched. This was real. This was bad. This wasn't negotiable. "Okay, okay," he grumbled, creeping into the open. "But when she eats me, remember it was your idea, and I hope you'll feel lousy about it." Slinking closer to the fence, he assessed the sleeping animal. She was big . . . mammoth, with a glossy black coat marked with tan. If there was anything he hated, it was waking things up, especially big things with teeth.

"Excuse me," Orie said, slithering through the fence and praying his luck would hold out.

Tenba flicked her ear but didn't respond.

The place where his tail had been itched, and Orie turned his head for a moment, gnawing furiously at the stump.

"This better be good," the shepherd mumbled, eyes now open, puffy from sleep.

Orie jumped with surprise and tried to speak. "I'm the liz—I'm the liz—"

"I know who you are." She yawned a huge, tooth-filled yawn.

Taking a deep breath, Orie prepared for the worse. "Look, I don't normally talk to dogs . . ." He stopped. That wasn't good—too confrontational. He decided to try again with a friendlier, more down-home approach. "Hey, neighbor, there's something I'd like to share—"

"What is it?" Tenba interrupted. She looked irritable—big and irritable.

"I am special. I was saved for great things," Orie chanted.

Tenba's lip trembled in a silent snarl. "I don't like it when you do that."

The lizard stopped, gave a friendly smile, and pictured the dog dead. It was a recurring fantasy he had with all potential predators, and it felt very soothing. Savoring the vision for another moment, he shook his head, then nodded graciously. "You're absolutely right. Anyone can see you're a no-nonsense gal, and I'll get right to the point. So here it is." He leaned forward. "I've had a dream. Sort of."

"A dream?"

"Yes, well, sort of a dream, only it's more like a feeling of . . . well . . . sounds."

The canine blinked.

"You know those cats, the ones Buddy's looking for? Well, I think they're in trouble."

"How do you know that?"

The lizard shifted uncomfortably. "How?"

"Yes, how?"

"Well, because I heard a thing in my head, of a cat in trouble, like a scream. Only it wasn't."

The dog stared.

Orie shut his eyes. Here was the part he'd been waiting for. She didn't believe him, thought he was nuts but edible, and was now preparing to kill him. His mind drifted to the corpse picture—rotting dog, one of his favorites.

"I believe you."

Orie opened his eyes. "Huh?"

"I said, 'I believe you.'"

"You do?" The near-death thing was getting old, and the

lizard felt cranky and drained. "Well, good, because I'm telling you it hasn't been all that great with this voice thing and all . . ." He trailed off, coughed self-consciously, and scratched his head. "So, anyway, that's what I wanted to tell you. Good-bye."

"Stop."

He froze, clawed foot extended.

"Something's going on," the shepherd said, struggling to her feet. "This is more than just cats being in trouble. This involves other species, and it's important. I felt it from the minute Buddy came into the yard." She stretched each back leg carefully. "We need to find them."

Orie leaped forward. "Where do you get this 'we' stuff? I've done my bit, I'm through!"

"But you're the one with the instructions."

"So?" Orie felt tired and hungry and wanted to leave.

"Then I'll need your help."

"For what?" he shrieked. "I'm three inches long, I don't have a tail, and I really haven't been feeling all that well. Trust me, you can do this alone!"

"But don't you see?" the dog persisted, moving closer. "Whatever this thing is, it's chosen you. You're the one with the information." She cocked her head, milky eyes intense. "Danger and desperation create powerful scents and sounds, and it looks like Mother has spread them farther than usual. I think you're hearing collective chatter from quite a few species who're trying to stop something bad from happening."

"Well, tell them to knock it off!" Orie exploded. "I've already tried the 'good deed' bit and, frankly, it was disappointing."

Tenba watched patiently. "I don't think you have a choice. I've only heard of this happening in rare cases, usually natural disasters, but I'd say something big is at stake if Mother has interfered. And besides" she tilted her head "you are *special*, right?"

Orie gaped in wonderment. Of course! Why hadn't he seen it before? It was Mother who had saved his life! Out of all the creatures in the world, She had chosen *him*! He scowled. But to help cats? It didn't matter. He was the key to salvation, the light in the tunnel, and possibly the most enlightened lizard in the universe! Orie allowed himself the teeniest squeal of excitement. Perhaps he'd become a famous evangelist, traveling the back roads, giving inspirational talks to the poor. He frowned. No, he'd never liked the poor; anyway, whatever his mission was, it should be more far reaching than that. He brightened. Global, with a lot of publicity—maybe even a tabernacle!

He turned to Tenba, his throat puffed with importance. "Of course I'll help," he said, his voice suddenly warm and paternal. "It's my calling, my destiny, my—"

"Good," the shepherd interrupted, kneeling in the grass. "Hop on."

A hollow feeling gripped Orie's stomach, and he staggered back. "What?"

"Time is important. Once I'm over the fence, I'm going to be moving fast." She paused. "And your legs are really . . . short."

Orie blinked in the morning sunshine, hoping he'd misunderstood. "You mean actually . . . on . . . you?"

"Yes. Hurry up; my knees are killing me."

"You know," he stalled, suddenly wishing he were back in the crawl space. "I probably should've double-checked my appointments before committing to anything . . ."

Do it! the voice screamed in his brain.

Filled with misgivings, the lizard touched Tenba's leg, took a shuddering breath, and scrambled over her shoulder, up her neck, and onto the surprisingly silky fur on her head.

The dog lurched onto all fours and coughed.

"Stop!" Orie shouted, tilting to the side and clutching her ear for balance.

"Sorry. Are you okay up there?"

Though hard to believe, he was. In fact it was thrilling to see the world from such a unique perspective. "Of course, I'm okay," he said in his haughtiest voice. "I've done this millions of times."

"Then hold on." With a grunt the dog leaped out of the yard, landing with a thud in the weeds. "We'll take alleys and back-streets as much as possible. I don't want to be reported as a stray."

Orie almost screamed with exhilaration as Tenba moved briskly toward the street. *If I've said it once, I've said it a million times,* he thought, relaxing in her soft ruff and tilting his face toward the sun: *I am definitely special and saved for great, great things.*

It was morning at Animal Control, and the big man yawned as he opened the door to his office. Muffled barking drifted from the kennels, and fluorescent lights flickered on above the dispatcher's desk. Picking up a clipboard, the man thumbed through some papers. "When did this come in?"

The dispatcher shrugged her thick shoulders. "What? The thing about the raccoon?"

"Yeah."

She frowned and thumped the paper. "It says right here, 8:00 A.M."

The man squinted, holding the report toward the light. "I can't read it."

"For heaven's sake, Curt, wake up!" Snatching it from his hands, the woman grabbed her glasses, skimming each word with a fat finger. "A guy says he killed what looked like a rabid coon last night. He dropped it off this morning, and it's in the freezer. Says it treed two cats, one yellow and a Siamese with some kind of shiny collar. They've probably been infected, we should look for them . . . and there's the address." She dropped it in his lap. "Plain as day."

Curt scratched his jaw and said nothing.

"Also, we had another call about the chow mix that's killing dogs in that same area, so it looks like you're going to be in Ryan Addition for awhile." She leaned back in the chair, her massive weight almost tipping it over, and grinned. "By the way, Judy's scheduled to ride with you today."

"Aw, man!" He banged the desk. "No wonder I can't get anything done! She doesn't do one freakin' thing but mess with the mirror and fool with that rat's nest she calls hair." He peered through the window, shielding his eyes from the glare.

A blonde woman dressed in Animal Control khakis lounged against a truck. A rat-tailed comb protruded from her hand as she probed her mile-high hairdo even higher.

"I'd worry less about her and more about your job," the

dispatcher sneered. "A reporter from the *Fort Worth Star* has already called asking about the chow thing this morning. People are wondering why we haven't found it yet. Better hope it doesn't hurt a kid, or—"

"Don't sweat it," Curt interrupted angrily. "I'll find him, and the cats . . . and, guess what? I don't care if they're rabid or not. We'll kill 'em *all* and save the city from a horrible epidemic." He belched with satisfaction. "Let the papers run *that*!"

SIXTEEN

SOMEONE WAS IN THE SHED. Buddy heard footsteps shuffling in the back of the building and the clatter of tools being knocked from shelves. He had no idea how long they'd been asleep beneath the lawn mower. Sun beat relentlessly through the open doorway, and the shed was hot and stuffy.

Feet clad in dirty tennis shoes passed by, and Shan Dara shrank back, body tense with terror.

"Where in the heck did I put that insecticide?" a man's voice mumbled as he rummaged somewhere above them. "I can't remember where I put anything anymore."

"Sam?" a woman called from the main house.

"I can't find it!" the man boomed, galumphing out the door. "I swear to God, Marie, can't you remember where *you* put anything anymore?"

A door slammed shut, and the two cats crept slowly from their hiding place and stood in the dusty silence.

"Is he gone?" Shan Dara asked, her eyes wide.

Buddy peered through the open doorway. "I think so."

A cat mewled in the distance, and their heads jerked up, nostrils testing the parched air for scents.

"Where did that come from?" Shan Dara whispered.

The two cats crept outside the shed and looked around.

"From next door in that old house," Buddy said.

Slinking closer, they peeked through the tangle of bushes separating the two properties.

"Does anyone live there?" the Siamese asked.

As if in answer, the screen door squeaked open and an old woman, holding a black cat, shuffled onto the porch. With great tenderness she placed the animal in a rocker, carefully adjusted its bandaged hind leg, and went inside.

"I'm going to get a better look," Buddy said. "Stay here." Crouching close to the ground, he slunk to the steps.

Simultaneously the black cat caught their scent and pulled itself into a sitting position.

"Who is it? Go away!"

"I'm not going to hurt you." Buddy stretched one paw toward the animal who struggled to jump from the chair. "I mean it, I'm not."

Twisting its head, the animal peered through the back slats of the rocker. "You can't stay; you've got to go." He looked with panic at the screen door. "I'm the only one here. She doesn't want any other cats. She only wants me."

Buddy studied the creature for a moment—dull fur, starvation, an injury. He knew the signs. "You're a Feral, aren't you?" he said softly.

"No! I'm not!" the cat shouted, trying to stand. "I belong to the woman. I'm an Indoor! Ask anyone!" The rocker tipped backward, and the cat fell heavily against one of the armrests. "Please go away. I found her first. She's mine."

Buddy jumped onto the porch. There was something about the cat's scent, something familiar. "It's okay, I know she's yours. I have a boy of my own." He stopped, grief and homesickness bobbing to the surface. "I mean . . . I lived with a family."

"Oh." The cat gave a knowing nod. "They dumped you out here?"

"No." Buddy glanced away. "It's a long story, but I'm not looking for a home. What's your name?"

"Soot." The cat's injured leg flopped awkwardly to the side. Flinching in pain, he shifted his position.

"How did that happen?"

"I was hit by a car. The old woman saved me."

"You're very lucky." Buddy inched toward the rocker. "Anyone can see the woman loves you—"

"Yes, she does," Soot interrupted. "She carries me everywhere, and we sleep together and . . ."

Buddy gently placed his paw on the back of the chair. "Believe me. You're safe now. It's okay."

A car honked in the distance, and they both jumped at the sound.

The black cat blinked. "I wasn't lying. I am an Indoor. I've been one for a whole day now."

He dipped his head shyly, and the gesture pricked Buddy's subconscious—something buried deep and long ago. "Congratulations on finding a home. I'm feral, too. Or, I was." Thoughts of the little house on Sixth Avenue, bright with love and safety, pulled at his heart, and he willed them away. "I'm wondering if you've seen some friends of mine. A calico and a white, long-haired male."

Soot started. "I saw them yesterday. They're traveling with a tom called—"

"Jett," Buddy interjected. "Where are they?"

The cat seemed confused. "I don't remember exactly what happened before I was hit by the car. No, wait a minute! We were running from some boys, and Pris was afraid to follow Jett across the highway."

"Highway?" Buddy leaned closer, ears alert. "Where?"

"Straight through the alley. There were cars coming, and Jett was yelling for her to follow him, but she just stood there. So I pushed her, and she ran, and—" His voice wavered, and he sighed with fatigue. "Then I was hit."

"What about the white cat?"

"I don't know. I don't think he was with us. We were trying to find food, and then the boys came." He dipped his head. "That's all I remember."

Buddy caught his breath. There was something about that gesture, that turn of the head. A bittersweet memory bobbed to the surface.

The air was crisp with fall, and he was a kitten, tumbling through piles of soft red leaves with a beautiful little tortoiseshell. She was gentle and sweet, and he was careful not to play rough because he wanted her to like him. They romped for hours in the fragrant foliage before he finally found the courage to ask her name. She dipped her head in that same shy way. "My name is . . ."

"Ahn-ya," he whispered, jolted back to the present.

When was the last time he'd seen her? How long had he been gone?

"What did you say?" the cat asked, startled.

Buddy walked to the front of the rocker and stared. "You're Ahn-ya's offspring, aren't you?"

Soot blinked in surprise. "How did you know?"

"I'm not sure. Little gestures I can't explain. I—I knew her once. Long ago." He took a deep breath, dreading the next question but compelled to ask. "Where is she . . . now?"

"Probably dead." Soot sighed. "The last time I saw her she was pretty sick."

Scents of baking cornbread wafted from the house, and puffy clouds lazed across the sun.

"What about the rest of your litter?"

"A chow got one, two were hit by cars, kids trapped the other. I'm the only one left."

Buddy stared into the sudden gloom, blinded by visions he'd never seen.

Bees dipped and buzzed amid the trumpet vines, and the cats sat in strained silence.

"So . . . are you headed to The Gathering?" Soot finally blurted. "I thought maybe I'd get to go, but it doesn't look like I'll be able to."

"Yes." Buddy remembered the vision of Ahn-ya by the pool and shook himself back to the present. "That's exactly where I'm headed." He considered asking about the old Cat Master's successor but was too ashamed to admit that he didn't already know. Wearily he rose on hind legs and touched the black cat's nose with his own. "I've got to go. I'm traveling with a friend, and she's waiting for me. Keep well. I'm happy for you." Jumping from the porch, he headed for Shan Dara's hiding place.

"Wait a minute!" the black cat shouted. "Who are you?"

The yellow tom stopped and turned. "Buddy."

Soot furrowed his brow. "That name sounds so familiar. I think my mother used to talk about you, only I can't remember what she said."

"It doesn't matter." Buddy averted his eyes. "I wasn't a very good friend."

"Oh, one more thing!" the young cat called, struggling to his feet. "That tom I was telling you about? Jett? You should be careful of him. He hates Zekki and Pris, and he's cruel. If you're going to stop whatever he's doing"—Soot swallowed hard—"you'll have to kill him."

Kill Jett. The thought wiggled in Buddy's mind, bright with truth. Hadn't he always known it would come to this? Isn't that why he'd stayed with The Boy, to avoid the very thing he was now racing toward?

Soot watched from the chair, his thin face anxious.

"Thanks for the warning," Buddy said. "I'll keep it in mind."

SEVENTEEN

PRIS HUDDLED AGAINST the trunk of a pecan tree and watched Jett sleep. Terrified to wake him, she had spent the night and half that day staring at his solid form, trying to recall what had happened.

There was a vague memory of an alley, the sound of cars in the distance, and voices screaming for her to hurry. She knew she crossed the highway with Jett, but after that, things became a blur. It seemed they ran forever, leaping fences, hiding in gutters, and even crossing a shallow creek before finally stopping in the grove. Now, crouched by the pecan's sturdy trunk, she felt dejected and alone in a way she had never dreamed possible. Where was Zekki, and how long had it been since they had walked through the doorway of their home and into this nightmare? She whimpered in distress, tail wrapped tightly around her body for comfort.

"Having a problem?"

The calico jumped.

Jett was awake and staring at her.

"I didn't really sleep much," Pris said.

The tom stretched and yawned, then slinked toward her, rubbing his head against her rump as he passed. "That's too bad."

A hot wind rustled the trees, and large green pecans plopped to the ground.

"I've decided to go back and find Zekki," she said, then cringed in fear at her audacity.

Jett swiveled his head. "You don't know?" The great eye drooped with sorrow. "I assumed you did."

Something in the calico's stomach knotted and rolled. "Know what?"

"As you ran across the highway . . ." Jett paused, voice sad and low. "How can I put this? Well, the boys that were chasing us? I'm afraid they caught him."

"Caught . . . him?" The words strangled in her throat.

"Yes, put him in a bag or something and took off. So sorry. I know this is upsetting, but you're in the Outs now, my dear. Friends don't last very long here, and you know how humans are." He peered beneath his brow. "Or do you?"

"But he was right behind me!" she sobbed. "I mean . . . wasn't he?"

The tom strolled a few paces and sprayed a pile of leaves. "Apparently not. If you still want to go back, that's fine, but you'll be going alone. I'll continue on as planned."

Zekki . . . gone? Was it really possible? Pris thought of his bright blue eyes and soft white fur and longed to drop into a warm cocoon of darkness and stay there. Though the loss was too great to imagine, the end result was clear. Before this, she'd never gone as far as the kitchen alone, and Zekki had always been there to protect and guide her. Now, if she wanted to go home, she'd have to do it alone. "I appreciate everything you've tried to do for us, but I—I think I'll just go on." Her words sounded foreign, and for a moment, she wondered who'd said them.

"Alone?"

"Yes, but—but, I'm sure Buddy is looking for us. He'll find me."

Jett's head snapped toward her. "Buddy?"

Pris blinked in confusion, one front paw tucked under her body. "I only meant—"

"I know what you meant." Jett's eye narrowed to a deadly slit. "You're waiting for Saint Buddy to save the day, aren't you? You've been counting on him the whole time." He crept toward her. "What's he ever done for you?"

The calico's mind blurred with terror, then jolted into perfect clarity. Jett was crazy.

Somehow, she'd always known it; a troubled feeling she couldn't articulate. But now, as he crouched before her, it was impossible to ignore.

"You know what you were before I found you?" Jett asked. "A fat, miserable blob staring out a window. Now look at you! Out! Free! Alive!"

"Thank you," Pris whimpered, desperate to run.

"Well, I've got big news, my dear." Slowly he circled her body, ears flattened to his huge head. "Buddy isn't going to save you. You know why?"

"Why?" she asked, voice quavering.

"Because he's dead, too."

"He isn't!"

"Of course he is! He's dead because he was soft like you and your insipid friend!" Jett hissed and lowered his haunches, ready to attack.

"Now isn't this a pretty picture?" a voice interrupted.

Jett froze, squinting upward.

A slender limb dipped and swayed above them, and two mockingbirds peered from the branches, eyes arrogant and bright.

The tom's demeanor changed, and he backed away from Pris. "Sorry. Domestic quarrel. Hope we didn't disturb you."

"Well, you are disturbing me." One of the birds sneered, flapping his wings. "Get out of here. This isn't your territory."

Jett crept toward a bush. "My mistake."

"Hey, he's only got one eye!" the male cawed derisively. "How many points for the other one?" He swooped from his perch, diving toward the tom.

"No!" Jett flattened in the grass, head tucked beneath his paw.

Pris tried to run for cover, but this time the mockingbird's mate fluttered above her, then delivered a ringing blow to the top of her head.

"That drew blood!" the bird screamed triumphantly. "Nice work!"

Fluttering to a branch, the two stared with impudence at the cats below.

"How did you like that?" the male cackled, jumping

from one foot to the other.

Pris scurried beneath a bush. A driblet of blood rolled down her face, and she smeared it with her paw.

"Hey, look at this." The bird landed on the ground in front of Jett. He did a cocky little hop toward the cat's head, then fluttered to the pecan tree. "What's the matter, freak face? You don't seem to be having fun."

Pris watched the big tom with amazement. Squirming against the ground, eye tightly shut, Jett groveled and mewled, making several attempts to run. Each time, the birds blocked his escape, swooping toward his head, pecking his ears, and coming closer and closer to his eye.

"I said we'd leave! I promise we'll leave!" he pleaded.

The female plummeted downward and hammered Jett's back. "Bingo! A direct hit!" she trilled.

"How many points for a blind cat?" her companion called. "Hey, kitty kitty, look at this!" With a whoop, he dove from the uppermost branch, zooming directly for the cowering tom.

Pris watched transfixed.

The bird gained speed, wings drawn close to his body, a gray and white projectile hurtling through space.

Suddenly Jett raised his head, pushed from his crouched position, and leaped upward.

The calico had never seen such speed and power. For one surreal moment, both animals seemed to be flying, the mockingbird desperately trying to alter his course, the cat arcing upward in an effortless interception.

With deadly precision Jett snaked out a paw, slamming the bird to the ground. It flopped in the grass, a bent wing dragging behind it. His mate screeched hysterically from the pecan tree. Diving toward the cat, she veered wildly to the left, finally fluttering to a branch where she perched in helpless anguish, beak open, panting with fear.

"Get out of here! I don't want you to see this!" the male called to her.

"No!" she quavered from her perch. "I won't leave you."

Tilting his tail up and down for balance, the wounded bird stared with open hatred at the tom. "You don't scare me."

"Your first mistake." Jett snarled, batting it with his paw.

The mockingbird fell backward, pivoting unsteadily to the left until he could see Pris. His bright black eyes locked with hers, straightforward and unafraid. "He lied about your friend," he said in a clear voice. "He's alive. They're all alive. We saw them."

"Buddy, too?" Pris started forward.

"If he's a yellow tom, yeah."

"Shut up!" Jett hissed. He swiped at the creature, nails extended, and sent it tumbling in the leaves.

A drop of blood rolled from the bird's eye and onto its beak. "Believe me. They're just across the highway." Turning his head toward the advancing tom, he spat on the grass. "Give it your best shot, freak."

Jett snapped its neck in one smooth motion, savagely shaking the body until gray and white feathers swirled in the hot air. The bird swayed limply in his jaws. Tossing it on the ground, Jett stared up at the creature's stricken mate.

"Bingo," he said. "I believe that was a direct hit."

With a tortured squawk, the female swooped into the hot blue sky. Behind her, a lone feather drifted from the pecan tree, settling quietly beside her fallen companion.

"Could he be telling the truth?" Pris asked, creeping forward. "Maybe they really are still alive!"

The tom rolled his eye in disgust. "Just how naive are you? Listen carefully." He spoke slowly, words brittle with sarcasm. "Birds are not our friends. Birds are dinner. Perhaps you've forgotten that hole she put in your head?"

"I know," the calico insisted. "But he said—"

Jett scratched a flea, broad face inscrutable. "I'd hate to think you believed one of them over your own kind."

"No!" Pris squeaked. "That's not true! It's just that . . . that . . ." She broke down, shoulders heaving, round belly jiggling with sobs.

Moving to her side, Jett rubbed his head against her shoulder. "There, there, my dear. What you need is nourishment. You're tired and hungry. Yes?"

Though repulsed by his touch, Pris stood in meek silence and nodded. Her mind whirled. If Zekki and Buddy were truly dead, then Jett was all she had, her only hope of getting home. He was dangerous, but so far, she hadn't been hurt. Maybe in some small way, he liked her and would spare her if she flattered his ego; stayed helpless and dependent.

He wrenched the bird's head from its body, licking the exposed flesh. "Ah, simple yet hearty." Pulling feathers from the chest, he ripped it open. "Would you care to join me or will you decline in deference to the great friendship the two of you shared?"

Pris wanted to run to the highway, shut her eyes, and race across it as fast as she could. But she was starving, and, painful as it was, maybe Jett was telling the truth: Zekki and Buddy might be dead; the bird lying to cause trouble. For the first time in her life, there was no one to depend on, and survival rested on her and her alone. An idea skittered through her mind. "Jett?"

He looked up, whiskers dripping with blood.

"Do you think The Cat Master might help me?" She moved closer. "As a favor to you?"

"I don't know," he murmured, voice vaguely amused. "Won't it be interesting to see?"

Sunset rouged the horizon, and glimmering shafts of light pierced the lush foliage of the pecan trees. Walking single file, the two cats passed through the grove and onto a gravel road. Moving to the side, they picked their way through ruts and ditches, staying close to the thick weeds that formed a fringe-like protection around them.

Pris watched Jett's powerful body as they walked. "I was confused back there with the bird and all," she called, voice breaking with emotion. "I don't know why I said those things."

Jett stopped and turned, face dark with suspicion.

Dejected, Pris stared at the ground. "Buddy and Zekki are . . . gone, and as much as it hurts, I have to accept that." She gazed up, her eyes wide and sincere. "I mean it, I'd be lost without you, and I appreciate your helping me."

"That's what I'm here for, my dear," Jett said, his voice pleased and relaxed. "You can always count on me." He paused. "And *only* me."

A gentle breeze ruffled the calico's fur, and a distant memory jostled for attention. What had Buddy said about The Wind if Pris was ever in trouble?

"Let's go." Jett turned briskly into a field.

Shifting from one paw to the other, she stalled. "Could you wait a minute? We haven't stopped in a long time, and I've got to . . ." she lowered her eyes "you know."

Without turning, Jett sat down, thick tail twitching in agitation. "Hurry up."

Moving out of his line of vision, she relieved herself on a clump of weeds. "I'm here, Mother," she prayed. "Show them." And for the first time in her careful little life, she didn't cover the scent behind her.

EIGHTEEN

ORIE SCOWLED AND TILTED HIS HEAD. Something was wrong with the dog's breathing. It sounded wet and strained. At first he tried to ignore it. When this didn't work, he sang all his favorite lizard songs as loudly as possible, but even that didn't blot out the gargled rumbling beneath him. Not only was the sound unnerving and irritating, but it also left him with a sensation that felt alarmingly like . . . what? He moved down the dog's neck, spit fur from his mouth, and wrinkled his brow in concentration. What was this thing he was experiencing? Was it friendship? No, that was way too simple. Could it be concern? Definitely not; concern was a prissy little word he had never related to.

Tenba stumbled, and the lizard felt a blast of emotion he could no longer deny. The feeling was sympathy. It was disgusting. Why should he care about the dog? He was saved for great things, not her. He made a mental note to stop feeling sympathy right away.

Tenba coughed, stumbling again.

"Stop!" Orie blurted.

"We're making good time," the dog gasped, continuing to trot. "Why?"

"Why? You're asking . . . why?" He felt suddenly ridiculous and groped for the right words. "Because . . . I'm feeling nauseous."

Tenba actually broke into a lurching cantor.

"Hey, it's up to you, but I had a fly before we left that looked a little iffy!" Orie moved closer to her ear and belched loudly. "Whoa, I can still sort of taste it."

The shepherd stopped. "Get off if you're going to be sick."

Orie made an ugly face behind Tenba's head and scuttled down her leg onto the ground. "I'm not sick."

Tenba was panting hard. Her sides heaved, and her long pink tongue hung from her mouth dripping saliva onto the pavement. "Then what's the problem?"

"I don't have a problem," Orie said, sidestepping a splattering droplet. "How about you? Do you have a problem?"

"Like what?"

The lizard glared. "Oh, the usual stuff. Fleas, ticks . . . bloody consumption."

"There's nothing wrong with me." With an annoyed grimace, Tenba looked away. "I'm just out of shape."

Orie squinted up at her from the sidewalk. He didn't know much about dogs, but this one looked more than out of shape. Her muzzle was gray, and her brown eyes had a milky film he hadn't noticed before. "I'm not stupid. What's the matter with you?"

She sat with a grunt of impatience. "Nothing. It's hot. I've been running. Do you want to do this or not?"

The reptile spread his legs. He was about to reply that no,

he didn't want to do this, and that if she wanted to kill her-self, it was up to her, when the voice-feeling unapologetically butted in.

Say yes.

It was the first time it had spoken since early that morn-ing, and Orie scowled, resigned to his lack of control. "Yes, yes!" he said, his voice slowly rising in volume. "I want to do this, but how about slowing down, for crying out loud?" He thought of his cozy crawl space and glowered with resent-ment. "You're shaking my guts out up there."

Tenba heaved to all fours. "I have to get as far as I can before dark. If I didn't have my collar on, I wouldn't have come with you at all. Too dangerous."

Orie stared at the worn leather collar with the dirty sil-ver tag. "So what's the big deal with that?"

"If I get picked up with it on, someone might take me home. Without it"—she gave a strained and bubbly cough—"well, you don't want to know."

"Sorry," the lizard said and was appalled to find he actu-ally meant it. "By the way, I can climb forty-foot trees, so you don't need to get on your knees." He scrambled up her leg back to the longer fur around her neck and made a clicking sound. "Giddy up, or whatever the heck they say."

"I'm sorry I was a little short with you," Tenba said. "Thanks for the concern."

"I'm not concerned," the lizard answered defensively. "I just wanted to make sure you weren't contagious." They moved in silence, and Orie listened carefully to Tenba's breathing. It sounded slightly better, and he felt an unwanted tickle of relief.

Traversing lawns, streets, and alleyways, the shepherd continued on, nose to the ground, snuffling for a scent that was fading quickly since the downpour of the day before. Finally, she stopped by a bed of sagging caladiums, eyes wide, tail high. "I've got it, and it's not far from here." She snorted. "Wait a minute; I'm picking up something else." Ears pulled back, she whirled so quickly that Orie was almost thrown from his perch.

A stray chow mix stood silhouetted against a boxwood hedge. It sniffed the air, then moved closer, its posture aggressive, its growl low and menacing.

The shepherd froze.

"What are you doing?" Orie screeched. "Get out of here!"

Tenba turned, tripping and stumbling up the sidewalk.

The chow cut across the street, his gate easy and unhurried. Orie could hear the rhythmic click of its nails on the pavement over the strained breathing of the shepherd. "Go faster!" he yelled. "He's gaining, he's—"

"Can't." Her front legs trembled with fatigue, and she staggered to a swaying stop. "Too tired."

"Not to worry, Fräulein," a cheery voice said from behind them. "I'm all over this."

A miniature Dachshund burst through the foliage, and the stray stopped in surprise.

"Get out of here!" The little dog's stubby legs churned through the grass. "This is my city, my street, my yard, and most importantly," he boomed, "that big fine bitch over there is my woman!" Sliding to a halt in front of the intruder, he snarled a quivering, white-fanged grin. "Now, beat it."

Shambling to the Dachshund's side, Tenba snapped and growled in an impressive sign of unity.

The chow eyed both animals, seemed to reassess the situation, and with a rumbling bark, galloped up the street and disappeared into a vacant lot.

Tenba sank to her haunches with exhaustion. "I don't know how to thank you."

"Oh, I'll bet we can think of something." The little dog strutted closer, eyeing her from head to toe. His lascivious sneer faded to surprise. "Don't be alarmed" his voice was low and conspiratorial "but there's a lizard on your head. Why don't I kill him for you?"

"No!" Tenba shouted, lurching back.

The Dachshund looked confused. "No?"

"No, he's a friend."

"A friend?"

"Yes, a friend! *Friend!* What are you, deaf?" Orie screeched from his perch above Tenba's left eye.

"Whatever." The Dachshund moved boldly to her rump, snuffling at her tail. "I'm Frank, and you are . . . ?"

"Looking for some cats," Tenba finished pointedly, moving away.

"Who isn't?" With a saucy wink, Frank continued his pursuit.

Orie's face contorted in disgust. "Geez, do I have to see this?" Slithering to the old dog's collar, he jangled the tags with impatience. "Could we please ditch Romeo and get moving?"

Tenba sat, her voice firm. "We're looking for some special cats. A yellow tom, a white longhair, and a calico."

"Oh, yeah, I've seen the yellow one," Frank said, pointed nose prodding her flank.

"You have?" Tenba fluttered her lip in subtle warning, and he stepped back.

"Yeah, I saw them from the window; he hooked up with our family cat. They took off over there and into that alley." The little dog suddenly seemed concerned. "Wait a minute. The cat's gone for good, right? I mean, she's not coming back?"

Before Tenba could answer, a door banged from behind the house, and a man ran into the front yard, clapping his hands with authority. "Frank, you bad dog, come here right now!"

The Dachshund rolled his eyes. "This has been going on all morning; I've already bitten him once. Watch this." Eagerly, he trotted toward his owner who squatted in the grass with arms outstretched, then veered left just as the man reached out to grab him. "Would love to stay, but you can see the situation here!" he called, neatly sidestepping another swipe of the big hand and sprinting in the opposite direction.

"Darn it, Connie, get the car keys. He's headed south!" the man roared.

"Thanks for the help!" Tenba shouted from the curb.

"Don't mention it!" Frank howled. "Come see me if you're ever in the neighborhood, and hey, bring your friend; I'm totally open-minded!" He turned a corner and was gone.

"How disgusting was that?" Orie muttered.

"Oh, I don't know." Tenba moved closer to the protection of the houses. "I think he had a certain charm." Scratching a flea with her hind leg, she assessed the sky.

Billowing white clouds lazed across the hot summer blue of afternoon.

"I figure we have about two more hours before we need to find some place to rest." She gave a shallow cough, noticed water dripping from a neighbor's faucet, and lapped thirstily from its rusted mouth.

"Now what?" Orie asked.

"Now we follow Frank's directions and find those cats." Tail high and nose to the ground, she trotted to the end of the block and turned left into the alley.

Shaking with rage, the chow watched from the shadow of a dying hackberry. The confrontation hadn't gone as expected, and being driven away by a smaller dog in broad daylight had triggered old feelings of rage and humiliation.

Flies circled a scabbing wound on his muzzle, and he shook his big head in irritation.

Everything would turn out all right. The snotty Dachshund was gone, and the old dog was obviously tired. Soon it would be dark, and the shepherd would be deep into the alley, vulnerable and alone. He could wait, he thought, squinting into the fading sunlight.

Waiting was his thing.

NINETEEN

ZEKKI SQUIRMED from beneath the rusted car, fatigued, hungry, and bewildered as to what to do next. Blood on the highway or not, Pris was out there with Jett, and he had to find her.

Something thumped on the hood of the car, and he dashed behind a discarded battery, ears scanning for danger.

Perched on the shimmering metal, black eyes fierce and unblinking, sat a mockingbird.

Intuitively Zekki froze in the grass, hindquarters tensed, ready to attack.

The bird watched impassively. "I know where they are." Her voice was flat and low.

Zekki stopped in mid-crouch, feeling confused and inexplicably frightened. "What?"

Scorching heat waved from the metal beneath the bird's feet, but she didn't seem to notice. "Your friends and the other one? I know where they are."

Zekki stumbled back on his haunches, queasy from stress. There was something strange about the bird. She didn't seem afraid, and yet all his instincts told him she should be.

Creeping into the open, he eyed her with a mixture of wariness and hunger. "Are they alive?"

"Yes." Her voice dragged with bitterness. "They're alive."

Relief shot through Zekki's body with such force, he winced. "Where are they?"

The bird fluttered from the car, landing boldly in the grass, and Zekki cowed back, trying to understand why she seemed so terrifying.

"I'll take you to them on one condition."

Zekki's throat tightened. "What condition?"

"That you kill him."

An ice-cream vendor rang a bell somewhere behind the alley, and children shrieked with delight.

"Kill who?" Zekki mumbled, knowing the answer before he asked it.

"Jett."

The cat's pulse drummed with rage. Who was this bird, and why had she asked such an impossible thing? He thought of Pris, and anger turned to shame. She was in danger, and the bird knew where she was . . . but to kill Jett? A malevolent yellow eye pierced his memory, and he cringed. "I—I wouldn't know how—"

"Those are my terms," she interrupted. "Take it or leave it."

"We'll take it," a clear voice said from the shadows.

Zekki spun in the direction of the sound.

Standing quietly in a patch of dappled sunlight, head erect, tail straight and high, was a familiar figure.

The white cat blinked hard, licked his chops, then sank to his knees, eyes vacant and dull. "I'm crazy," he muttered.

"I've gone crazy, and I'll never see Pris again."

The specter moved closer. "You're not crazy. It's me."

Zekki peered dully through a haze of shock. "Buddy?"

"Yes."

"Buddy?" he repeated slowly, struggling to his feet.

"Yes, you're all right. Everything's going to be okay."

The young tom took a tentative step, then rushed to his friend, falling before him in trembling submission. "It's my fault! Pris wouldn't have left the house if it hadn't been for me! Jett! He—he lied to us! What if Pris is hurt? I'm so glad to see you, how did you find me?" His words tumbled out in a torrent of anguish, guilt, and relief.

Buddy licked the young male's ear and nudged him to a sitting position. "I'll explain everything to you later." He turned his attention to the mockingbird who'd fluttered to the car. "Where are they?"

"How do I know you'll kill him?" Her eyes were hard and unblinking.

"You don't. You'll just have to trust me."

The bird hesitated for a moment, then sagged with defeat. "They're beyond the pecan trees across the highway. I can show you."

"Thanks for the offer," Buddy said. "But you've given me all the information I need."

With a listless flap, the bird rose into the sky. "He killed my mate!" she shrieked, circling higher. "Avenge him . . . for me!"

Her mournful words hung in the smothering heat, and the two cats watched silently until she became a small black dot on the horizon, finally disappearing from view.

"I almost forgot!" Zekki cried. "There was blood on the highway! I saw it! What if—?"

"It wasn't Pris," Buddy said quickly. "It was Soot. I just spoke to him. He's fine. A woman rescued him."

"Can I come out?" a voice called from behind the car.

Zekki bristled in alarm.

"Don't worry, she's a friend," Buddy said. "Yes, come out."

The Siamese peeked around the rear bumper, then stepped gracefully over a discarded battery.

"Shan Dara," Buddy said, "this is Zekki. One of the cats I've been looking for."

Zekki stared in awe.

The beautiful Siamese brushed his shoulder with her cheek. "I've heard a lot about you. I'm glad you're all right."

The white cat gave a sheepish nod, then turned to Buddy. "I don't understand anything that's happened. I mean, who is Jett, anyway? Why did he pretend to like us?" His voice broke with the betrayal.

Shan Dara's blue eyes widened. "What's Zekki talking about?"

Buddy took a long, deep breath. "Jett's my brother. I don't have time to explain everything right now, but he hates me and always has. I think he's used Zekki and Pris to lure me into the Outs."

"But why?" the Siamese asked.

"He wants to kill me. He's tried it before. That's when The Boy rescued me." The tom shrugged with frustration. "I wish I could give you more details, but I don't completely understand it myself."

Shan Dara and Zekki stood in stunned silence, their unspoken questions floating like specters in the hot August air.

"What do we do now?" Zekki finally whispered.

"We go back and see if Soot will find us something to eat. Then we cross the highway."

"Cross the highway?" The young cat's mind flashed to the smell of melting tar and the roar of traffic. An unknowable shadow waited there, something evil. "I can't do that."

"But you will," Buddy said. "Fate never takes no for an answer."

TWENTY

JETT STOOD ON A HILL overlooking the golf course. He hadn't seen it in years. The alley where he'd been born was only blocks from here, and he and his brother had been drawn to the plush greens and fascinating sand traps of the course. Jett surveyed the landscape. Nothing had changed. Enormous oak trees swayed above the clubhouse, golf carts squatted in tidy rows, and a man-made pond sparkled behind the ninth hole. As kittens, he and Buddy had spent an entire autumn playing by its edge. That's when they had first seen Ahn-ya. Abandoned and terrified, she had instinctively turned to them for protection, and Jett was instantly smitten. Considered the more handsome of the brothers, the gray tom was normally confident around females, but there was something about the tortoiseshell's winsome innocence that reduced him to awkward mumbling. Not Buddy. His affection toward Ahn-ya was open and natural, and she responded to him immediately. For a blissful time, the trio was inseparable, exploring the orchard, stalking birds, and spending hours stretched side by side in the warm fall sun.

But slowly Ahn-ya and Buddy's bond deepened, creating a world in which there was room for only two. Isolated from his brother and rejected by Ahn-ya, Jett watched with longing from the lengthening shadows. Never before or since had he felt such stark and aching loneliness.

Something wet rolled alongside his nose, and Jett was shocked to see a teardrop dangling from his whisker. Quickly he shook it off, replacing the memory with hatred. *They weren't kittens anymore,* he thought bitterly, *and things had changed.* Jett took a hard look at the sky. He and Pris had traveled the better part of the day, and with evening approaching, they needed a place to sleep. He watched the calico struggle up the slope. She'd been uncomplaining and obedient, eating when he said to and resting only when he did. Unfortunately she had also been surreptitiously marking a trail since leaving the pecan grove, and he was going to kill her. Not because of the trail—he'd been marking one himself since the first day they'd met—and not because of her pitiful attempt at deception, which he'd actually found impressive if naive. No, he was going to kill her because her usefulness to him was almost over. All he'd ever needed was a clear scent for Buddy to follow . . . and the brainless calico was supplying that daily. Unfortunately for her, that trail was coming to an end.

"Can we stop here?" Pris gasped, pulling herself up the last incline and collapsing by the tree.

Jett swiveled his head to the side and stared, his one eye hard and glistening. "Oh, I think we should push on a little farther. There's a place I know that would be safer for us to sleep." She looked disappointed, and he tried not to laugh. "It's not far. You've been a real trooper, and when we get there, I promise you'll be able to sleep for a long time."

"Really?"

She gazed at him with that fat-faced sincerity he was beginning to loathe.

"Oh, yes," he said. "I'd say a very long time."

She gave a theatrical yawn, trying to appear casual as she always did when she was working her little plan.

"I think I'll just look around for a minute, if you don't mind."

"No problem." Jett smiled. "Take as long as you like." The irony was wonderful. He couldn't believe how well everything was turning out.

A butterfly lit on a clump of lantana, and he swatted it down, holding it carefully beneath his paw. Only one little thing bothered him: where was Buddy? The yellow cat had definitely fallen for Jett's plan because the mockingbird had seen him. Tipping his head, Jett squinted into the afternoon glare, hoping Mother would send Buddy's scent. There was no breeze, and scorching air parched his throat. Scowling, Jett put more pressure on the insect's body, enjoying the feeble movement against his pad. Could it be he'd forgotten something? His tail twitched in frustration. The abduction had been flawless, the stupid calico would die, and eventually her dumber friend would, too. No, he had done a splendid job, no mistakes. But time was running out. The Gathering would be tomorrow night. What if he'd miscalculated again? What if Buddy had taken a different route and was lurking in the shadows, watching them right now? A wild panic fluttered in the gray cat's chest, and he struggled to breath. No. Ambush wasn't Buddy's style. If he were here, he'd make his presence known. Everything was just taking a little longer than expected. Slowly Jett's pulse returned to normal. *He could wait*, he thought, ripping off a delicate orange-and-black wing and swallowing it whole. Patience never failed a true believer.

Curt and Judy jiggled and bumped down the alley between Sixth Avenue and Willing, uniforms stained with sweat. The Animal Control truck's air conditioner clattered in disrepair, and they had rolled down the windows to stave off the heat.

"Now where were these cats supposed to be?" Judy asked, pushing her bangs off her dripping forehead and balancing a snare in her lap.

"They were first sighted between Fairmount and Fifth; then they ran toward Willing. At least that's what the report says."

"Well, heck," Judy said, "no telling where they are now."

They rocked along in silence, slowing down to stare under bushes or behind rubbish piles for any signs of life. Once, two black-and-white kittens scurried under a chain-link fence, eyes wary and alert, but the cats they were looking for were adults.

"Didn't the guy say the Siamese was the one with blood on her?" Curt popped his gum and steadied a Big Gulp cup he kept gripped between his thighs.

"Yeah, but those coons are fast and mean, especially when they're rabid. I wouldn't be surprised if it got the yellow cat, too." Judy coaxed the top of her towering hair even higher with a pencil, then looked at her watch. "Geez, Curt. It's almost six thirty. Can we please get the heck outta here? I'm burning up!"

With a squeal of tires, Curt turned the truck and cut through a mall parking lot. "Yes, your freakin' majesty," he muttered, swerving to a dumpster and tossing his Big Gulp cup inside. "Think you can hang on till I call the office?" Punching a number in his cell phone, he put it to his ear. "Hey, it's me. Listen, we've been out all day following up on that report about the rabid cats somewhere around Sixth Avenue . . . No, we didn't see 'em, and we're headed back . . . Yeah? Wait a minute." He grabbed a pen and began scribbling on a worksheet lying on the seat between them. "On Fifth? Another attack by the chow? Listen! Don't start with me . . . Yeah? Well, I don't care what they . . . how would I . . . shut up!" He finally bawled, pounding the dash. "I'm talking here! What do ya think we've been doing all day, picking daisies? We've gone all through that neighborhood, and we didn't see a thing!" Judy started to speak, but he stopped her with a look, then pressed the receiver close to his lips, face red with fury. "Hey, if the mayor thinks he can do a better job, let him come out here and try! And, by the way, tell that freakin' reporter there's no freakin' rabies epidemic in Fort Worth!" Clicking off the phone, he threw it to the floorboard and stared sullenly through the window. "I'm gonna get that chow and those cats tomorrow, and then you know what I'm gonna do?"

"What?" Judy said, blotting her lipstick on a gas receipt.

"I'm gonna drive straight to the office . . . and put 'em down myself."

The possum crept from beneath the dumpster as the truck roared away. He had just finished off three cockroaches and half a tub of margarine when he heard the truck rumble up.

Scuttering into the darkness, he'd remained motionless as he listened to the people talk, hoping they'd leave. The sun still smoldered on the horizon, and usually he slept as late as he could, but he was familiar with the sound of the Animal Control truck. It was one of the few things that actually worried him. Moving further into the open, he watched as taillights turned a corner and disappeared in the murky twilight.

He'd seen lots of animals go that way. Sometimes the back of the truck, the part with the locks, seemed about to explode with all the panting and whining. Once the Animal Control people had even snagged a possum. He'd seen it. It had been bad. He snuffled the pavement where the tires had been. Fear and urine. Yep, it was definitely them.

What had the man said about cats? Bits of conversation drifted back. A yellow cat, cats in alleys, a cat looking for other cats. It had a familiar feel somehow. He sat down with every intention of giving this some real consideration, then spotted a rat slinking toward a melting dip cone by the curb. He'd think about the cat thing later. Scurrying across the warm asphalt, he stared at the sticky remains with rapture. "You gonna eat that?"

The rat squeaked in surprise and scrambled under a loading dock.

"I'll take that as a no!" he called. Turning his attention to the ice cream, he slurped and grunted with pleasure. Maybe he'd wander up to the highway and check out the garbage bins on Willing.

With a happy belch, he waddled across the parking lot, long pink tail gliding behind. A horn honked in the distance, and he jumped under an abandoned shopping cart. There was something about those cats that sure rang a bell. Maybe if he had time later, he'd figure it out. His eye caught the glimmer of a candy wrapper. On the other hand, he reasoned, trotting toward the oozing confection and licking his chops, he hated wasting a lot of energy on anything he couldn't eat.

TWENTY-ONE

BUDDY, SHAN DARA, AND ZEKKI crisscrossed yards and side streets until they finally reached the old woman's house. Creeping through the bushes, they approached the structure with wary curiosity. Cicadas yammered with monotonous insistence and tangles of cross vine dragged at the screened-in back porch.

"Where's the food?" Zekki sagged against the bottom step for support.

"I don't know. We'll ask Soot." Buddy's eyes strained in the darkness. Something didn't feel right, and he wanted to leave as soon as possible. "You and Shan Dara go back to the shed next door and wait for me."

"Why can't we just stay with you?" the Siamese demanded, eyes drooping with weariness.

Buddy playfully nudged her head. "Because I think you'd be more comfortable in the shed. Listen, Shan Dara, every-thing is fine. Just give me some time to find Soot; he'll take care of us."

"I'd rather stay with you." Her slender jaw tightened.

"I know you would, but do what I'm asking, okay?"

She stared unblinking. "You'll be back soon?"

He nodded. With an exasperated sigh, Shan Dara turned toward the toolshed, Zekki trailing behind.

Buddy watched until he was sure they had found the opening through the hedge, then began to parole the perimeters of the house. A dim light shone through a back window, and he jumped onto a broken lawn chair, stood on his hind legs, and steadied himself on a ledge. Through the screen he saw the old lady sleeping. She lay on her back, mouth slightly open, a sheet drawn over her chest. An oscillating fan hummed on a dresser, and there, curled against her neck, was Soot, his injured back leg resting gently across her shoulder.

The lawn chair beneath Buddy shifted in the dirt, and the black cat jerked awake, eyes glowing. "Who is it?" he hissed in the darkness.

"It's Buddy. I need your help."

Jumping off the pillow, Soot limped to the window and peered nervously through the screen. "Are you alone?"

"No. I'm with Shan Dara, the Siamese I've been traveling with, and Zekki."

"So, you found them?"

"Only Zekki. Pris is still with Jett. We need to rest and eat before we go on. Do you have any food?"

Soot's pulse throbbed. He did have some food left in the little bowl the woman had been setting out for him, but he'd have to let the cats inside to eat it. What if the woman woke up? Maybe she'd be mad, blame him for disturbing her, decide she didn't want him anymore. Or worse—his heart began to thump—what if she liked them better? He pictured himself back in the alley, crippled and alone.

"Do you have any food?" Buddy repeated.

Soot swallowed hard. "I think I ate it all." His words hung in the air like ashes.

A car screeched around a distant corner. Tejano music blared from a boom box.

"I see," Buddy finally said. He leaped from the chair, and the black cat heard the rustle of dried grass as he retreated into the darkness.

Soot huddled on the bedroom floor, his stomach churning. That had been wrong. All cats were brothers, and he'd betrayed them, lied to them. He needed to bring them back, offer them everything he had. Hobbling toward the kitchen, a hard pain in his leg brought him to a panting stop. Leaning against the wall, he slowly limped past the sleeping woman, down the hall, and to the screen door. Gritting his teeth, he put his full weight on both back legs and pushed hard against the frame. As she often did, the old woman had neglected to lock the door, and it creaked open an inch. "Don't go!" he called, stumbling out on the first step. "There's plenty of food for everyone!"

"That's really nice of you," a voice said behind the bushes. "Where?"

Soot jumped backward, squalling with pain. "Who said that?"

"I did." Ambling to the foot of the steps, the possum sat

down, scratched behind his ear, and waited for what he thought was a polite amount of time. Finally he cleared his throat. "So where is it?"

The cat looked confused. "Where is what?"

"You know . . . the food."

"Food? You mean the food for my friends?"

The possum inspected the moonlit yard, face twisted with confusion. "What friends?"

Soot followed his gaze. The yard was empty with only an occasional firefly to break the velvety blackness. He slumped on the steps. "You're right. What friends? I don't have friends because I don't deserve to have them." He stared in misery at the toppled lawn chair where Buddy had been. "How could I have done that?" he muttered, limping back toward the door. "Buddy was hungry, Pris is lost, and Zekki—"

"Lost?" the possum said. Something was coming back. Lost cats. Cats in danger. "Is one of them yellow and the other a Siamese?"

Soot stopped, face blank with amazement. "How did you know?"

"Animal Control is looking for them. I heard them talking by the dumpsters."

"What? Why?"

"Don't know . . . something about them being bitten by a rabid raccoon." He remembered the smell of the tire tracks and suddenly longed for the security of the loading docks. "They'd better hide. The man sounded mad; said he's gonna kill them."

Soot leaped onto the grass with a moan. "Buddy!" He hopped toward the alley on three legs. "Zekki!"

A wave of paranoia gripped the possum. "Wait for me!" he shouted, running after the black cat's retreating form. He stumbled in a snarl of honeysuckle that separated the alley from the woman's backyard, its tendrils grabbing his feet and tail, its aroma light and sweet. "Wait!" he called again, breaking free and scurrying beneath a young cottonwood tree for protection. A sudden breeze gusted through its branches, and he froze. There was evil in the air. It was a dank and nauseating smell, and he gagged from the stench.

With a squeal the possum bolted into the alley. *Something was wrong with this place,* he thought, sprinting after Soot.

Something was terribly wrong.

TWENTY-TWO

THE SKY HAD DIMMED to amethyst twilight, and Pris's sides heaved with fatigue. She and Jett had been walking for hours, and he still showed no signs of stopping. "Can't we just rest for a little?" she cried. Her muscles ached and her stomach gurgled with hunger.

"It's not much farther." He sounded happy. "We're almost there."

The golf course was immaculate and lush. Jett had cleverly avoided the men in carts, crouching in weeds amid halos of gnats until twilight forced the last golfer home. Sprinklers came on, and the cats lapped thirstily from the spigots, water spraying in all directions, the fine mist clinging to their coats and whiskers.

"When are we going to eat?" Pris called, as they crossed a velvety green and slogged through a sand trap. The big male appeared not to have heard, and she finally sat in frustration. "Please stop. I can't go any farther without food."

Jett turned, and she flattened to the ground, tearful and afraid.

"You know what?" he said, his huge head close to her face. "You're absolutely right; we do need to eat."

"We do?" She looked up in surprise. He didn't seem mad at all. In fact, he seemed pleasant, exuberant even.

"If you can manage a little farther, there's a place over behind that house that always has food out for cats."

"You mean we're going to a real house where people like cats and there's food in bowls?" She couldn't believe her ears; maybe she would get home after all!

Jett chuckled softly. "Well, not exactly in bowls, but I think you'll like it. Come on, I'll show you."

Together they trudged through the wooded area that encircled the course, then entered the back of a well-lighted yard.

Pris stared in awe.

The house was grand, with two stories and a balcony that overlooked the sculpted greens. Apricot roses dripped from an arbor, and planters of impatiens, ferns, and purple sweet potato vines created a fairyland of scent and color.

"Who lives here?" she whispered.

"Like I told you, people who love cats." He took a deep breath. "Can you smell the food?"

The calico gave a timid sniff. At first all she discerned was the sweetness of flowers and damp earth, but there was definitely something else. She inhaled deeply, her little nose red with the effort. "I do! I smell it!" Her mouth watered. "What is it?"

"See for yourself." Jett moved closer, whiskers grazing her ear. "It's right over there."

Together they crawled through the underbrush separating the house from the golf course. The scent became stronger, and Pris pushed ahead, salivating with anticipation. "I can't find it!" she wailed, sniffing the ground and bushes in a frenzy of hunger.

Jett walked to a clearing and stopped. "It's here, but be careful. There's a pretty steep drop on the other side of those bushes that goes straight down to a creek. I wouldn't want you to get hurt."

Pris ran to where he stood.

A rectangular wire box glimmered in the moonlight.

The calico crept toward it, cautiously sniffing again. "But where's the food?"

Jett strode with confidence to the far end of the contraption and sat down. "There," he said, indicating a scoop of tuna glistening just inside the wire. "All you have to do is walk in and eat it."

"Are you sure?" Pris inched closer. "I've never seen food in something like that."

Tail flicking with irritation, the tom frowned. "Are you hungry or not? If you are, eat it. If you're not, we'll keep going. It's all the same to me."

Pris hesitated for a moment, then walked to the opening of the cage and inhaled. The smell rose in oily waves, strong and irresistible. She raised one snowy paw, then stopped. "But aren't you going to have some?"

Jett plopped beneath a clump of dandelions and yawned. "Of course I will, but you go first. I need to rest for a minute."

The calico stepped gingerly over the rim of the wire. It was narrower than she had originally thought, but not a problem once she got used to it. The open can was at the opposite end, and she carefully navigated the wire passage until it was almost in reach. "I can't get to it!" she said, stretching her neck as far as she could.

Jett's voice rose with encouragement. "Of course you can. Just move forward a little farther; you're practically there."

Pris took another step. "Wait a minute." She started to back out. "This doesn't feel right." Her paw made contact with a small metal plate, and something slammed behind her. She whirled, astonished to find a mesh wire door now blocking the entrance to the box. Frantically banging against the sides, she screamed as a hook snagged her ear. "Help! I can't get out!"

Rising to his feet, Jett sauntered to the cage, rubbed his eyeless socket against the wire and peered in. "You're right."

"Can't you help me?" Tears spilled down the little female's cheeks and onto her chest.

He glanced at the trap and shrugged. "I don't see how."

Exploding in panic, Pris thrashed against the enclosure, banging her head into the wire and kicking the metal until she finally stopped, bruised and trembling. "But this is a trap!" Her racking sobs penetrated the sudden quiet. "You said the people loved us."

"Oh, they do love us," Jett said, stifling a laugh. "They love us . . . dead." He went to the end of the cage, snaked a paw through the wire, and pulled out a hunk of tuna, which he gulped in one bite. "Here's a little secret." His voice lowered to an intimate purr. "Humans don't like cats running free and sharing their world." He licked oil from one claw. "They only like fat, dull cats that they can keep as prisoners for their amusement." He grinned, his teeth white in the moonlight. "So, they set traps, and stupid cats get caught, and then the nice people come and kill them."

Pris shrank against the side of the cage, horrified.

"But don't worry," Jett said, snagging one more helping of fish. "That won't happen to you."

A flutter of hope pulsed at Pris's throat. "It—it won't?"

"No," he said, carefully cleaning his whiskers. "Because they're not going to be able to find you." Leaning his full weight on the wire, he pushed hard.

The trap lurched forward, and Pris toppled to her side. "What—what are you doing?" she screamed, fighting to regain her footing.

"I'm pushing you over the side of the cliff." The big male reared on his hind legs and thrust forcefully against the cage. "I wouldn't want the nice people to find you . . ." he grunted and pushed again ". . . before our hero does."

The trap moved easily over the short grass, then stopped on the edge of the embankment, the front end teetering into space. Beneath her, Pris could hear rocks tumbling down into the darkness, and the gentle burble of water. Crouched motionless, her breathing rasped with terror. "Why?" she whispered. "Why are you doing this?"

"Because you've served your purpose, and because of the clever little trail you've left, I don't need you anymore. But let me take a moment to thank you. Your pathetic dreams of adventure have lured the sainted Buddy into the Outs, where he's now racing against time to save you." Twisting his head, Jett smiled without humor. "What a surprise to find me instead."

Pris blinked back tears. "Please, please, I don't understand."

156

"I'll put it as simply as possible." Jett pushed his face so close she felt hot breath on her fur. "He stole my destiny, and now I plan to take it back."

"But you said he was dead!"

"He's not dead." The great eye glittered in the moon-light. "You are!" With a grunt he slammed the cage with one massive paw, howling with laughter as it toppled over the embankment, bouncing end over end into the chasm below.

TWENTY-THREE

THE GERMAN SHEPHERD stood at the mouth of the alley, head up, nostrils probing.

"Well?" Orie asked, moving to sit between Tenba's eyes. "Anything interesting?"

"I've got them. I mean, they're really close." The dog gave her body a head-to-tail shake, which sent the lizard soaring over her nose and onto the ground.

"That was a nice thing to do. Thank you," Orie said irritably, shaking the dust from his back and flexing his hind leg. "And by the way thank you again; I think I've sprained my foot." He took a tentative step. "No, it's okay."

Tenba gave him a sniff. "Sorry, sometimes I forget you are up there." She sat down and coughed. "Okay, you need to get a little more specific. Exactly which cat were we supposed to help? Mother's sending a lot of different smells."

Orie wrinkled his brow. "I don't know. I only heard a cat scream once, then I was directed to you." He noticed a moth on a drooping briar and flicked his tongue with pleasure.

"I smell Buddy and some other feline scents, so I guess

we'll go for that unless you're told something different."
She paused. "Well?" she said louder.

Orie jumped, and the moth fluttered into the bushes.
"That's great," he groused. "I just lost dinner. Well, what?"

"Has the 'feeling' given you any more instructions?"

The lizard concentrated hard. "I don't hear anything, so
I guess that means we're doing the right thing, whatever the
heck that is."

Both animals sat silently in the darkness. Rats scuttered
through garbage pails, and a grasshopper popped out of the
grass and onto Tenba's ear. She shook it off and began to
pant.

The old dog had been much better since the sun had
gone down. Her heavy breathing had been only intermittent,
and each time it started Orie made an excuse to stop so she
could rest. "Boy oh boy oh boy!" he said too loudly,
scratching his itching stump and giving a dramatic yawn.
"I'm pretty darned bushed. We know where they are, and
we don't have any more information anyway, so why don't
we just settle down somewhere, get a little sleep, and start
fresh in a couple of hours?" He gave Tenba a sidelong
glance, trying not to notice the froth collecting at the cor-
ners of her mouth.

She nodded, licking her chops. "I'm thirsty. I think I'll
just wander down the alley and back to the street. Maybe
somebody has a sprinkler on or something." Heaving herself onto all fours, she trudged heavily toward the curb.
"You stay here; I'll be right back."

"What, are you kidding?" Orie screeched, scurrying to
where Tenba stood and clamoring up her hind leg onto her

back. "I'm not staying here." He looked fearfully over his shoulder. "Did you see those rats? One of them gave me the 'look.' Forget about it, we're staying together."

Sitting quietly between her shoulder blades, the lizard enjoyed the thick, sweet smells of the summer night. Fading roses clung to fences, and vegetable gardens sprawled, spent and yellowed amid the last barrage of August's heat.

In the next block they found a child's plastic swimming pool. Orie dropped from Tenba's muzzle onto its rim, and once in position, both animals drank for a long time from its bright blue depths.

"I feel a lot better," the shepherd announced, waiting for the lizard to scramble onto her back.

"Yeah." Orie gagged, spit, and furiously wiped his mouth on her fur. "I always find kids' pee very refreshing."

Tenba ambled back toward the protection of the alley, turning warily into its unknown murk. A faint spill of moonlight illuminated a cluster of bushes growing behind a garage, and she stopped. "This look okay?" she asked, legs already folding onto the dry grass.

"Whatever you think." Orie plumped up the fur at the base of Tenba's tail and cuddled into the curve of her bony hip.

Groaning with fatigue, the dog curled into a tight ball and closed her eyes.

Orie waited until he was sure she was asleep, then carefully crawled across her flank, rooting his head beneath her fur and pressing his ear to her ribs.

The old dog's heart thudded with an obviously irregular beat, and the wheezing had returned.

Something twisted in the lizard's gut, as he listened to each ragged breath. He didn't like the sound of it. He didn't like it at all.

The chow watched from the shadows. An abscess, oozing pus and blood, festered on his jaw, and his whole head throbbed with a feverish heat.

He'd followed the German shepherd all afternoon and was glad she'd finally stopped to rest. Dogs barked in the adjoining yard, and he was confident his scent would mix with theirs if the wind should change. The old bitch had been talking with the lizard. They were looking for cats, and it appeared they'd almost found them. This altered his original plan somewhat, but it didn't matter. He would still get her; it's just that he'd kill the cats first to start his juices flowing.

A soft breeze smelling faintly of rain wafted through the night air, and the chow lowered himself in the brown grass. He ignored his aching wounds and shut his eyes. His thoughts drifted to the man and the little girl, which often happened when he was tired. It was an obsessive theme that he played over and over in his mind. He wasn't sure why he did this, because it was painful and confusing. Maybe it was a way of keeping his connection to the girl alive, or maybe it was to fuel the hatred he now felt for the man and his kind. Either way, he relaxed, letting the visions unfold.

He remembered the car, its engine running, its interior jammed with suitcases, kitchenware, and boxes. The man was angry, which wasn't unusual. "Shut up, Brenda; I'm not going to tell you again!" he screamed, grabbing the child's arm and shaking it hard. "He can't come with us! I told you I'd find you another dog when we get settled!"

Brenda's small hands clutched his ruff, holding it as tightly as possible, but the man pulled her away, swung her into the car, and they roared off. Crying, the girl waved through the back window, her eyes huge and sad. The chow chased them for a few blocks but couldn't keep up, so he'd returned to the empty house.

It wasn't clear how long he sat in the driveway waiting for their return. Papers piled up on the sidewalk, and people walked boldly to the front door, peering through curtainless windows, as he barked uncertainly from the bushes.

They hadn't returned.

After that, things had changed.

Boys threw rocks instead of balls, and food came in garbage cans instead of bowls. It had taken awhile to understand that humans were no longer his friends and that the little girl was gone. But he wasn't stupid. He remembered the last words the man had said: "I'll find you another dog."

They were going to replace him. Somehow he must have broken some very important rules, and because of that he'd been left behind.

He decided to make some rules of his own. First: the world was his personal territory. Second: anything that crossed his path was trespassing, and Third: anyone caught doing this would pay the ultimate price. The last edict he particularly enjoyed because it allowed him a righteous outlet for the anger always bubbling beneath the surface. His victims didn't need to understand why. The world bulged with unknowable rules, and those who broke them needed to be punished, just as he had been.

A child's laughter drifted from a house, and he sprang to his feet, whining.

Not Brenda, of course, it never was, and for some reason, as he stood in the stifling darkness, that knowledge made him hate the world just a little bit more.

TWENTY-FOUR

THE MOCKINGBIRD PERCHED on the skeletal branch of a dying oak, ignoring the sour smells of rotting leaves and algae from the creek below. Beneath her, the trap lay on its side in the mud, the front half in the stream with at least two inches of water lapping around the cat's crumpled form. Hoping for a better look, the bird swooped to the top of the cage, landed lightly on its rusted rim, and squinted through the wire.

The cat was alive, though its head was twisted to the side, and its eyes were staring out in shock. Seeming to sense the bird's presence, the calico tried to speak, "Zek—Zek." The sound was garbled and faint.

Tilting her head, the mockingbird pecked at the wire. "Can you hear me?"

Pris stared blankly into the darkness. "Zekki?"

"No, it's not Zekki, but I know where he is." She hopped to the very end of the cage, speaking as loudly as possible. "He's not too far from here, and the other cat, Buddy, is with him."

The calico shifted and winced. "Buddy," she repeated dully.

"Yes, the yellow one. He's with your friend. They're on their way to find you."

Pris's eyes opened wide. "No!"

The bird fluttered backwards in surprise.

"No! Go back, Zekki!" Pris called into the darkness. "Jett's waiting! No! No, run . . ." Her words trailed into incoherent mumbles, and her eyes stared in dazed confusion.

Flapping to a branch, the mockingbird watched with concern. The cat was either hallucinating or crazy, and both were afflictions the bird understood. Life had become foggily surreal since her mate's death. She had hardly eaten or slept since his murder, and had spent a day and night soaring through the orchard calling his name. That was before she had seen Jett on the golf course. After that, she obsessively followed him, his movements feeding a dark curiosity she couldn't explain. At first she watched his callous behavior toward the calico with detachment, because they were cats, and she despised them both. But it became increasingly clear the two weren't alike. The female appeared gentle and nonthreatening, and Jett acted as cruel to her as he did to everyone else.

Pris gave a feeble kick, and the trap listed further into the creek.

Even in the moonlight the bird saw the water rising around the cat's head. Soon it would cover her face, and she would drown. The bird ruffled her feathers and considered her options. Buddy had promised he'd kill Jett, but why should she really trust him? Her black eyes narrowed. Perhaps she could use the whereabouts of the calico as insurance; make sure Buddy kept his word. Of course, he'd said he knew where to find Jett, but would anyone think to look in the creek behind the ravine for the calico?

Owls hooted in the distance and sprinkles of stars glimmered and winked through wispy clouds. Had it only been two days since she'd soared with her mate in the orchard? Forcing her mind to the present, the bird shook her head. Already a smoky dawn pushed through the darkness, and she needed to have a plan.

The cat coughed and gagged below. Flying to a lower limb, the bird watched the cage as it shifted farther into the creek. A slight wind rustled the weeds along the ravine, lifting a slender sycamore branch. For an instant, a bright shaft of moonlight illuminated the trap.

Leaning forward, the bird gasped. The door had sprung open from the fall, and though the opening was very small, it was no longer locked. "Hey!" she called, "the door isn't fastened! You need to turn around and try to push it open!"

There was no answer.

"The trap is sliding into the creek. If you don't hurry, you're going to drown!"

Pris lifted her head, trying to pull herself upright, but the effort appeared to be too great, and she flopped back into the pooling water.

Mosquitoes buzzed in the stillness, and the oak tree creaked with decay, leggy limbs stretched skyward.

Squawking in frustration, the mockingbird peered into the gloom. The cat drifted in and out of consciousness and wouldn't be able to hear unless the bird got as close as possible. Fluttering to the ground, the bird moved toward the submerging cage, her white-rimmed wings held away from her body. In a flurry of water, she skimmed over rubble and onto a clump of rocks jutting from the creek. From there she hopped from one precarious perch to another until she was almost even with Pris's head. "Wake up!" she screamed, leaning as far as she dared toward the cage. "You need to wake up!"

A frog splashed beside her.

Startled, the bird slipped on a glistening patch of algae and teetered into the creek. A tangled swirl of leaves dragged her tail beneath the surface, and she strained to keep her wings from following. In her frantic struggle she almost didn't see the long dark form drop from an overhanging branch and land with a plop to her right.

The gaping white mouth of a water moccasin rose from the water.

It was in striking position and looking at her.

"What do you mean he—he didn't have any food?" Shan Dara stammered in disbelief. She stood in the doorway of the shed, her fur bristled with anger. "I don't believe that! Zekki is so hungry he can barely stand. Indoors always have food around!"

A car door slammed, and a woman's drunken voice shouted from the house next door.

The cats scurried beneath a workbench. Wide-eyed, they listened as an engine revved, its escalating howl drowning unintelligible conversation.

"Let's get out of here," Shan Dara hissed.

Buddy sat quietly, ears cupped back, whiskers fanned. "Wait."

Squealing tires roared up the street, their shrieks blending with a cacophony of barking dogs, and a screen door banged close.

"Everything's okay." Buddy moved into the open. "It's over." He turned to the Siamese crouched in miserable silence on the dirt floor. "I know you're hungry."

"Me?" she protested, standing up. "I wasn't talking about me, I was talking about . . . I'm not at all . . ." Her voice broke, and she sagged to the ground. "All right, I was talking about me. I am hungry. I'm just so hungry." Periwinkle eyes filling with tears, she looked at Buddy. "You said Soot was a friend."

"He is a friend. Right now he's a frightened friend, but he'll do what's right. You'll see."

"I don't know why you're so sure of that."

"Because," Buddy said, walking to the doorway of the shed and staring into the night. "He's my son."

Shan Dara gaped in astonishment.

"Your son?" Zekki moved from the corner of the shed.

"I knew Soot's mother, Ahn-ya, since we were kittens." Buddy sighed, reluctant to tell the story and yet knowing it was time. "I told you before that Jett tried to kill me. We fought, and he pushed me into a dumpster and left me to die."

"But you're brothers! Why would he want to kill you?" Shan Dara asked.

Buddy furrowed his brow, trying to put feelings into words. "I've never really been sure. We were as close as kittens. But something began to change around the time we met Ahn-ya."

"I'll bet he was jealous." Zekki gave a knowing nod.

"Yes, he definitely wanted her." Buddy drew a deep breath, realizing how vulnerable Ahn-ya had been in his absence, and how cruelly Jett had taken advantage of that. "But it was more than jealousy," he continued. "It was true hatred, as though I was out to hurt him in some way. As though . . ." Buddy paused. "As though my being alive was something he couldn't bear."

The cats stood in the quietness, their breathing soft and barely audible.

Buddy cleared his throat, suddenly self-conscious. "Anyway, after Jett pushed me into the dumpster, The Boy heard me crying for help and rescued me. It was really hot that day, and I was in pretty bad shape." He sighed. "So The Boy took me home. I'd been feral all my life . . . and I'd never even been touched by a human before, but The Boy was"—his voice cracked—"The Boy was so good, and he needed me." He remembered Tenba's words. "What I mean is we needed each other." Buddy hung his head. "It's hard to admit, but for awhile it worked. I forgot all about the alley . . . well, not exactly the alley, but the trouble I'd had there. At least, I tried to, though I couldn't have left, anyway, because all of us were kept indoors. I love The Boy . . . but . . ." He sighed again. "It's hard to explain."

"I don't understand," Zekki said. "We all loved The Boy. Why was that so bad?"

"You were born an Indoor, Zekki. The feral world is so different. Feral law allows cats of the alley to use humans as survival tools only, as a source of food or shelter. But it's considered treason to actually live with them."

"You didn't plan for this to happen," the Siamese protested. "You were traumatized. Anyone would have chosen a loving home over the alleys, and you said yourself you weren't allowed outside."

Buddy's eyes were dark and unreadable. "It's more complicated than that."

Zekki crept to Shan Dara and lay down. "What about Soot?"

"I knew Ahn-ya was going to have our litter when The Boy found me. I kept thinking I'd find a way to get back to her." Buddy paused, his thoughts shameful and dark. "No. I *should* have found a way back, no matter what it took . . . but time passed, and I started thinking of myself as an Indoor . . ."

"But you were. What's so terrible about that?" The Siamese's face shone with encouragement.

Buddy clenched his jaws, suddenly unwilling to continue. "A lot of things. Anyway, I sensed Soot was mine as soon as I saw him. He doesn't know it. He doesn't need to, not yet."

The aroma of freshly mowed grass swept through the shed, and the cats raised their heads, checking for danger beneath its cover of sweetness.

A familiar scent floated beneath it.

"Isn't that . . . ?" Zekki started to say.

Something clattered in the distance, and a voice called "Buddy!" from behind the shed.

The cats prepared to run.

"Stay here." Buddy crept slowly out the door and headed toward the old lady's house.

"Where are you?" the voice called again.

Footsteps thrashed in the brush, and Buddy shrank into the shadows. "Soot? Is that you?"

The black cat crashed awkwardly through the honeysuckle, his injured back leg tucked tightly beneath his body, bleeding. "I've been looking for you everywhere," he panted, breath ragged with fear.

Obviously, this wasn't about food, and hackles rose on

Buddy's back. "What is it? What's wrong?"

"Animal Control is looking for you two. You've got to go. They drive around here all the time."

"Where did you hear this?"

"A possum told me. He overheard them describing two cats that look just like you and Shan Dara. The man said they'd been bitten by a rabid raccoon." Soot stepped back. "You weren't, were you?"

"No."

Soot sighed with relief. "That's good, but you still need to get out of here, because it's not like they just want to pick you up." His voice quavered. "They want to kill you."

"Thanks for telling me."

Soot's leg shook from fatigue, but he stood firm, head up, expression straightforward. "I lied about not having any food. I don't know why I did it, but I do have food, lots of it. There's a whole bag on the mud porch and—"

"Help!" a panicky voice screamed from behind him.

Soot leaped sideways, and Buddy bared his fangs.

The possum stumbled into the clearing, sides heaving, tail carried high over his back. "It's coming; let's get out of here!" He backed against a cluster of ferns, lips parted, teeth exposed.

Soot looked confused. "It's the possum I was telling you about. He—"

"Do you smell it?" the frightened creature interrupted, crouched in the dirt, staring upward.

"Smell what?" Soot asked.

"In the air!" The possum cringed, mouth opened wide and hissing. "Mother's warning us! There's evil coming, and it's close!"

A soft breeze cooled the night, and the first leaves of

fall drifted around Buddy's paws. "Yes," he said, "it is." He turned toward the possum. "Don't be afraid, it's not after you."

"How do you know?" The possum shivered.

Buddy stood motionless, moonlight bathing his face in a silvery haze. "Because it's looking for me," he said softly. "It's always been looking for me."

TWENTY-FIVE

THE MOCKINGBIRD SCRAMBLED BACKWARD, her wings whipping fine sprays of water against the snake's head as it struck. Venom spattered her breast, the deadly droplets opaque among her fine feathers, but the fangs missed their mark, grazing a mound of twigs instead. Undaunted, the snake continued forward, tongue flicking, body a zigzag of black in the ebony water.

With a squawk of desperation, the bird struggled to become airborne, tail still dragging with the weight of leaves and debris.

"Look! Look over here!" a weak voice croaked from the trap.

The snake stopped and raised its head, turning its attention toward the cage where the cat struggled to stand.

Water and mud sifted around Pris's paws as her movements propelled the trap further into the creek. "Hurry, while it's looking at me," she called to the bird, falling back onto her side.

A puff of clouds drifted across the moon, temporarily

washing the creek in gloom. With a last burst of energy, the bird pushed up from the water, fluttering to the oak whose brittle boughs waited like an old friend. Breathlessly, she clung to the rough bark, panting with exertion. "Thank you!" she finally called to the cat, flicking the last tangles of weeds from her tail. Shock rolled through her mind in a dreamy fog, and she fought to shake it off. "I know where your friends are." Her voice was weak but determined. "I'm going for help!"

Pris raised her head, and the trap inched forward in the mud. "Please hurry," she groaned, falling back against the wire floor.

The mockingbird held tightly to the branch and looked down. Beneath her, a linear shadow moved in languid ripples through the water.

Stopping for a moment, the snake stared upward, its hooded eyes flat and unreadable, then proceeded smoothly toward the cage, moonlight glittering on its supple back like diamonds.

Shan Dara stood outside the shed door, body tense, one paw lifted up and trembling. There were voices by the old lady's house. She recognized Buddy and Soot's, but she wasn't able to make out the other. There had been fear and urgency in the muffled conversation, and she was feeling more frightened by the minute.

"What's happening?" Zekki peered from beneath a saw-horse just inside the door.

Feeling his anxiety, Shan Dara rolled in the dust, trying

to appear relaxed. "Not much. I think Buddy's talking to Soot. He'll probably be back any minute."

"Oh." The white cat let out a long breath and returned to his hiding place. "I hope he's found some food."

Moving cautiously from the doorway, Shan Dara peered into the shadowy bushes separating the shed from the alley. "Oh, I'm sure he has. That's probably where they are right now." She inspected the area.

Heavy shrubbery stood between the main house and shed, and the fact that no one could look out the windows and see them gave the Siamese a slight sense of security. The salty smell of fried chicken drifted in the evening air, and she slumped with hunger and homesickness. No longer an Indoor, she suddenly understood what Buddy had meant. She was now in the Outs, where life was measured in hours and days, not months or years. Never again would food and water magically appear in stainless steel bowls or humans be a source of safety. For one panicked moment the Siamese considered running home, then gasped with an unexpected revelation; she already was. Buddy was her home and had been since the first time they'd met. Whatever unspoken burden he carried would be shared by them both, and she saw their futures entwined like morning glories, tough but beautiful. Her thoughts turned to Zekki. His protection fell to her, in Buddy's absence, and she took the job seriously. "I'm going to stretch my legs," she called, careful to keep her voice even and smooth. "Just walk around a little." There was no answer. Trotting back to the shed, Shan Dara squinted into the darkness. "Okay?"

Something moved by the alley, and she jumped, banging

her flank against the door. It creaked and swayed on its hinges. "Buddy?" she called, voice quivering.

"Buddy?" Zekki echoed from the shadows. "Is it Buddy?"

"No," she answered, heart lurching. "It was just a mouse or something."

The rustling sound grew louder, and the bushes to the side of the shed jiggled slightly, releasing a soft sprinkle of yellowing leaves. She shrank back. "Who is it?"

A gray face with a pointed nose peered through the foliage. "Are you Shan Dara?"

She nodded warily. "Who are you?"

"Possum," he said, waddling toward her, his face friendly and benign. "Buddy said to tell you he's with Soot getting some food. We're supposed to wait here until—"

A branch snapped behind him, and the Siamese froze in terror. "Run!" she screamed, but the gaping jaws had engulfed the possum's hindquarters, tossing him hissing and twisting into the air.

The thing in his mouth was not a cat.

This was a surprise to the chow, and he didn't like surprises. With a savage snap of his head, he shook the possum, who had stopped struggling and now swayed limply in his mouth. Snarling, the dog flung it to the ground, where it lay quiet and unmoving amid a clump of weeds.

The chow felt the electric jolt of adrenalin that always followed a kill. Perhaps this hadn't been such a bad thing after all. Perhaps it was a warm-up for things to come.

Howling with exhilaration, he listened as the sound reverberated through the alley.

The Siamese had run into the shed, and he galloped toward the doorway, sniffing the dusty air. She was there, and she wasn't alone. A flash of white bolted from beneath a sawhorse, scrambling to a ledge by the window, and the chow lunged inside, leaping high against the wall.

Paint cans tumbled from shelves, and the white cat frantically twisted beyond the dog's jaws, finally springing backward onto the ground, where it writhed among scattered tools, trying to regain its footing.

"Run, Zekki! Go!" a voice shouted from behind him.

Instinctively the chow whirled, realizing in an instant he'd been tricked. The white cat sprang out the door, and the Siamese clamored to the rafters, where it now watched, safe and out of reach.

A yellow cat he'd never seen stood solidly in the doorway, fur bushed, ears flattened in warning. "You want to kill something?" it asked. "Try me."

Infuriated, the chow lunged, missing its mark as the yellow cat dashed into the darkness, stopping between a pile of lumber and a thick row of nandina. Eyes blazing with fury, the cat arched its back, emitting a low and threatening yowl.

The dog pawed the ground with pleasure. He loved a good fight, and this cat seemed tough. He moved closer, aware the feline had backed itself into a corner. With a hiss, the cat swiped at the stray's muzzle, razor claws leaving a thin line of blood in their wake. Undaunted, the chow shook his head, yipped with delight, and prepared for the kill.

Something pounded up the alley, the sound getting closer and closer, and both animals froze with confusion.

The tom's expression changed from rage to surprise, and before the chow could turn, a massive form crashed against him from behind, knocking him to the ground. Stunned, the chow stumbled to his feet and stared into the livid face of the German shepherd. He blinked, mystified. How could this be happening? The old bitch could barely walk. This kind of strength was impossible!

The yellow tom sprinted away, and a dark premonition pinched the chow's consciousness. Things were going very wrong. Slowly he circled to the left as the growling shepherd followed him, saliva dripping from her jaws, canine teeth gleaming white against purple gums. He snapped at her foreleg, but she moved with surprising agility, and he felt her teeth clamp onto the ruff beneath his throat. Desperately he bucked beneath her grip, straining for release as they tumbled in the grass, bodies locked in a tangle of dust and fur. He could hear the old dog's wheezing grunts as she stumbled to her knees, their savage snarls primal and deadly.

Something burned white hot as she worked her jaws against his skin. Twice he threw her to the ground, his fierce struggles and brutal thrusts wrenching her neck, but still she hung on, fangs now deeply imbedded and dripping with blood. Flesh tore beneath her grinding attack, and he shrieked in pain.

Without warning, she released her grip and let go.

The chow tumbled backward, then rolled awkwardly to his haunches. Shaking his head, he gave a choked cough.

Inky arcs of liquid spurted onto the ground, and he noticed with surprise that they were coming from his throat. The shepherd had vanished in the blurry glow of moonlight, and he blinked with confusion at the flecks of color swimming before him. Maybe the cat had run back to the shed. In slow motion he looked around. Two pairs of gleaming eyes stared from the bushes. He tried to stare back, but couldn't hold their image in focus. A car's engine roared in the distance, and staggering to his feet, he tried to locate the sound. Could it be Brenda and the man coming back for him? Maybe they hadn't found another dog after all!

Lifting one paw as if to turn, he collapsed against the shed door, his weight pushing it shut with a slow and mournful creak. A soft breeze ruffled his fur, and he stared in dreamy fascination at the warm black blood pooling around his head.

In the misty distance a little girl called his name.

Wagging his tail, he closed his eyes, surrendering at last to oblivion.

TWENTY-SIX

ORIE STUMBLED THROUGH THE WEEDS, his breathing shallow, his chest tight with fear. Knots of brambles pulled at his legs, and his heart thudded with each step. Things had happened so fast, it was hard to put them in order. He remembered going to sleep in the alley, then awakening to the sound of howling. Tenba had struggled to her feet, shaken him to the ground, and simply said, "I've got to go."

At first Orie jumped back onto her flank, screaming all sorts of arguments for staying together. Temba listened patiently until they both heard the low, unearthly cry of the cat echoing in the distance. "Be safe," she said, giving him a gentle nudge with her nose, and then she was gone.

Keeping close to the fence line, Orie moved slowly, his flicking tongue trying to taste Tenba's scent particles. An unexpected breeze made them easy to locate, and he ran three blocks into another alley before he heard the snarls and screams of dogs fighting in the yard beyond the fence. The sound reverberated in his head, and he cowered in shock, paralyzed by the intensity.

Above him raccoons rustled in a fig tree, and the lizard dove beneath a rumpled sack, eyes peeking from its greasy folds as he listened in horror to the distant battle. Garbled growls rose in volume, followed by a strangled yelp of pain, then silence.

An eerie calm descended on the alley.

The coons waited a beat, then crashed to the ground in a flurry of twigs, struggling over a fence into an adjoining yard.

Orie stayed hidden until their steps no longer crackled through the weeds, then crept into the open, his heart pounding with a dread he couldn't name. To his right a streetlight shone on a rotting fence covered with wisteria, its woody vines twisted and gnarled against a weathered gate. Slithering through a narrow crack, he darted toward some honeysuckle, then stumbled against something soft and unmoving. The unseeing eyes of a possum gazed upward. Beetles marched across its snout and blood congealed in clumps on its tail.

With a gasp, Orie skittered toward the shed in panic, diving beneath a fallen rake and blinking at the scene before him.

Three cats stood in a semicircle staring at what appeared to be the body of a dog. Orie sensed the creature was dead, and the cloying scent of blood was thick and unmistakable. Something horrible had happened here . . . something unspeakable.

"Not Tenba, it's not Tenba," he whispered, but a hollow feeling of doom uncoiled in his gullet, rendering him mute.

Taking a deep breath, he willed himself to look at the dog. The body was turned away with only its back visible in the murky light. He squinted, eyes watering from the strain, and slowly recognized the figure. The tail was curled, its color pale, the fur long and matted. It was the chow! He sobbed with relief, and the cats snapped their heads toward the sound, eyes wild and glimmering.

One of them was Buddy.

"It's me, Orie! The lizard in the crawl space!" he shouted, praying the cat would remember him. "I'm right here by the shed! Don't let anybody eat me, okay? I'm coming out! Here I come, okay?"

"Leave him alone," Buddy said. "He's a friend. Come on, Orie."

With halting steps, Orie moved into the moonlight, aware of the frozen stares and the tails that twitched with agitation. "I've been . . ." he stopped, swallowing hard. "I mean, Tenba and I have been looking for you."

A thin black cat limped furtively into the bushes, and a white one, vaguely familiar, crouched behind the chow, fur bristled.

Terror closed Orie's throat, and he fought for air. What was he doing? Since when were cats to be trusted? Fear drenched his body. This is what happened when you mixed species, making friends, exposing yourself to impossible dangers. A sudden vision of Tenba's soft brown eyes filled his mind. He stopped, shocked at the jumbled emotions that followed. *It didn't really matter what happened to him*, the feeling seemed to be saying. *The important thing was to find Tenba*. This idea was so unfamiliar, he wondered if it was the voice that had just spoken and not his own thoughts at all.

Cocking his head, he listened intently.

Wind rattled the hackberry, and a train rumbled in the distance, its whistle lonely and sad, but there was no voice, only the steady sound of his heartbeat.

The white cat shifted its position, and Orie started but stood his ground. "We were asleep in the alley and heard a dog howling, then a cat scream." He blocked the mental picture of his friend struggling to her feet. "Tenba said she was going to help. She ran in this direction, and that's the last I've seen of her." He looked at the chow. "Dead?"

"Yes," Buddy said, stepping forward. "She killed him."

Orie tried to speak again, to ask the question gnawing at his heart, but his tongue stuck like a withered worm against his palette.

The cat's golden eyes held his. "Over there," he said gently, indicating a stand of bushes.

The lizard cleared his throat. "Is she . . . is she . . . ?"

"Orie?" a weak voice croaked from the darkness. "Is that you?"

He scrambled toward the sound, his pulse throbbing in his ears. "Yeah, it's me! I'm coming!"

Tenba lay in the grass, her sides heaving with labored breathing.

Scrambling to her head, the lizard peered into one liquid eye, relieved to see a flicker of recognition. "Are you okay? Are you hurt?"

She gave a wheezing cough. "Can't get up . . . hard to breathe."

"Hey, you're just tired, you're okay." He patted her

muzzle with a trembling claw. "All you need is some rest; you're going to be fine." Looking fiercely at the cats now watching from a respectful distance, he puffed his throat for emphasis. "She's okay," he said too loudly. "You guys can go on. She's fine, she's okay . . ." His voice broke, and he took a gulping breath.

"Orie?" the dog croaked.

"I'm right here."

"Do I . . ." she shut her eyes with the effort ". . . do I still have . . . collar?"

Orie stood on tiptoe and peered at her neck. "Yeah . . . I can see it."

"Tags?"

Pushing under her head, he burrowed into the soft mass of fur bunching around her throat and fought the urge to stay in its comforting warmth forever. The tags were splattered with drying blood, but they were intact. "I'm looking at them. They're right here." He tapped the metal heart with her name engraved on the side, then withdrew, crawling onto her foreleg.

She drew a deep breath. "That's good."

A dry wind swept through the grass, and Orie longed for water.

Buddy approached the shepherd, stopping at a respectful distance. "Thank you, Tenba. You saved our lives."

The shepherd seemed not to have heard. Her eyes were partially closed, her breathing shallow and slow.

Icy dread arced through Orie's heart. "She's okay," he lied, searching the cat's eyes for hope. "She's going to be fine."

Buddy averted his gaze, then scanned the sky. "We've probably got about three hours until daylight, and we need to eat." He paused, glancing at the motionless dog. "One of my friends was trapped inside the shed when the chow fell against the door. I'll stay here until I can figure a way to get her out, but I'm sending the others on ahead after they've eaten." Moving closer to the lizard, he lowered his voice. "I think you should head home while it's dark; it'll be safer."

Orie gaped in disbelief. "Go home?" he shrilled. "Are you kidding? Leave her here alone? No way. I don't know how you guys operate, but we travel together or we don't travel at all!" His voice quavered. "She's my friend."

"I understand," the cat said quietly. "She's lucky to have a friend like you."

Orie blinked and said nothing.

"Be careful, then, and good luck." Buddy trotted toward the shed, the other cats trailing behind.

Turning to the shepherd, Orie patted her nose, but she didn't respond. Fighting tears, he stumbled into the darkness and paced in the dust. How had this terrible thing happened? How long ago had the feeling come to him, and where was it now? "Mother? Where are you?" he screamed, face upturned, challenging the dark and silent sky for an answer. "We did what you told us; we trusted you!" Even as the words left his mouth, he knew them as lies. Never had he felt trust, not for the voice, not toward anything. But Tenba had. She had never questioned it. Never questioned him. Shaking in anguish, his body pumped up and down in despair. "You can't do this to me!" he shrieked into the blackness. "I'm special. I'm special and I was . . ." He stopped and looked at the dog.

It seemed to Orie a sudden brightness illuminated her body, the light so bright it hurt his eyes. Creeping closer, he stared in awe. The voice-feeling was back, and though nothing was audible to him, he knew it spoke to Tenba. She lay as he'd left her, legs outstretched as though running, great head resting on its side, eyes slightly open. She let out a long, even sigh, and Orie saw her body twitch and then relax.

With a cry, he clamored onto her jaw, entwining his claws in her whiskers. "You are special!" he sobbed, tears rolling down his snout and dripping onto her muzzle. "And you were saved for great, great things."

Stars faded in the indigo sky, and feathery clouds drifted toward dawn.

Zekki and Soot sat silently by the porch while Buddy stood watch by the shed, talking quietly with Shan Dara through a crack in the door.

The chow and possum lay where they had fallen, and the lizard slept the gray sleep of grief, face buried in the warmth of his friend, who lay in the darkness, her peaceful eyes open and fixed on the moon.

TWENTY-SEVEN

JETT LOLLED BENEATH a stand of ferns overlooking the creek. A trio of doves cooed in a nearby sycamore, and he watched them hungrily, finally deciding food could wait. He had been monitoring Pris for most of the night and was delighted with how things were unfolding.

At first he had worried the trap would slide into the creek immediately, and then, of course, there would be nothing to save when the valiant Buddy finally arrived. But no, once again Jett was reminded that right was on his side; otherwise, how could one explain the fabulous irony of the mockingbird? Natural enemies, pulling together, each helping the other in time of crisis. How high-minded, how newsworthy, how perfect for what he had in mind. And now, spunky and heroic, the mockingbird was flying to find Buddy. Perhaps the moronic Zekki would come, too.

"I know where your friends are," she had said.

"Good," Jett thought darkly. "Godspeed." Rubbing his damp socket in the grass, he groaned with pleasure. The

187

dewy air smelled fresh despite the sourness of the creek, and he flipped belly up, enjoying a rare moment of exuberance that left him uncharacteristically optimistic. Yes, the bird had been a wonderful surprise, but not nearly as much as the snake. What unbelievable luck! He squirmed in the sweet foliage, vigorously twisting his back in the twigs and inhaling the pungent aroma of marigolds drifting from sculpted gardens by the course. Flipping to his feet, he leaned farther over the ravine.

Beneath him the cage remained visible in the murky shadows of dawn. The cat had revived somewhat. She still lay partially in the water, but her head was slightly up, eyes open wide. Straining forward, Jett could see that the snake had made its way to the cage and was now twining itself around the metal handle at the top. Maybe it was looking for a way in. He considered the dramatic impact of this turn of events: death by drowning or death by venom. He snickered. Poor, fat Pris; hard decisions for a creature with such limited abilities.

A gust of wind blew a smattering of leaves over the creek, and Jett jerked his head to attention. A multitude of scents floated in the air, but not Buddy's. Disappointment soured his mouth, and frowning, he fought a bittersweet memory.

Spring transformed the alley. Tender green shoots pushed through decay, and mimosas dripped with pink blossoms, their fallen petals drying in ruined sweetness on the ground. Winter had been cold, and his mother stretched in a welcomed sliver of sunshine, watching her kittens play.

Behind her a black-and-white tom sat in the shadows. He was small, thin, and bent with age, but, even then, Jett had sensed the old cat's power. Spellbound with longing and hungry for a recognition he couldn't name, Jett desperately searched for a way to be noticed by the stranger and finally decided on a plan. Choosing the runt of the litter as an unwitting partner, Jett attacked it with gusto. What had started as a simple demonstration of strength and agility quickly escalated to full-blown aggression. With a snarl, Jett grabbed the kitten by the throat and shook it hard. Blood spurted from the wound, and suddenly the thing in his mouth was no longer his sibling, but prey. That's when things had gone wrong.

"Let go! You're going to kill him!" a voice had shouted from behind. "If you want to fight something, try me!"

Surprised, Jett had turned to see Buddy, normally so passive and quiet, now bristled with anger, his paw raised to protect their weaker brother. Confused by the challenge, Jett had turned toward his mother for help. She avoided his gaze, but the stranger's face was dark with disapproval, and Jett suddenly realized he'd made a terrible mistake. For the rest of the day, he had watched in misery as the old cat's eyes followed Buddy's every move. There had been pride in the stranger's expression, and something more. Jett didn't fully understand the importance of what he had sensed, but one thing was clear: Buddy was his enemy. Looking back, the tom was surprised he hadn't realized it before. First, Buddy had stolen Ahn-ya, and now he'd shamed Jett in front of everyone, including the powerful male whose approval he'd so desperately sought.

By morning the black-and-white tom had vanished, but

Jett had never forgotten the commanding stranger or the harsh lesson his visit had taught: Jett could survive only if Buddy was dead.

Jett hissed at the memory. It had only been the first of many humiliations handed out by his brother, each one greater than the last. But the tide had finally changed in his favor. Even the great Cat Master made mistakes, and the proof of that would be clear to everyone very soon. "Patience," Jett intoned softly. "Patience." With a slow, calming breath, he looked once more over the ravine.

A delicate dawn melted into the hazy blue of morning, and in the creek beneath him, the snake slithered over the top of the cage. Flicking its tongue against the mesh wire, it appeared to change its mind. Slowly it climed onto a low-hanging branch, coiled amid the foliage, and waited.

The mockingbird awoke with a start. For a moment she blinked in confusion, trying to understand where her mate was and why they weren't in their nest in the pecan grove. Slowly the memory of his death surfaced, and depression split her heart like a cleaver. But something else nagged, too. The cat! The cat lying in the creek! She squinted into the cobalt sky with horror. How could this have happened? The last thing she remembered was resting for a moment—that's all—just closing her eyes for the tiniest of seconds, and now it was morning!

Flapping her wings, she soared skyward. From her vantage point she could see where the pecan grove ended and a thin line of highway began, separating the alleys from the golf course and beyond. Pinpointing the area where she'd last seen the cats, she swooped closer to the houses lining the neighborhood.

It couldn't be too late; it just couldn't be.

Buddy sat on the shed's windowsill, looking inside through the cracked and dirty panes.

Shan Dara's worried face stared back. She touched her nose to the glass. "You've got to get out of here before those people find you."

"Stop saying that; I'm not going to leave."

Something landed on the tin roof above them, and both cats crouched low, eyes wide and curious.

The mockingbird peered over the edge, breathing hard. "Buddy?"

"It's me." Buddy stood on his back legs, sharpening his claws on the rotting wood. "What are you doing here?"

"I've found your calico friend, and she's in trouble."

He stopped, ears forward. "Where?"

"In a trap that's sliding into a creek by the golf course. I think she's hurt, and there's a snake." She hopped closer, her ebony eyes bright with fury. "Jett did it; he pushed her. I saw it."

Buddy turned to the Siamese pressed anxiously against the glass. "There're some things I have to do. The bird's found Pris, and she's in danger."

"Wait!" Shan Dara squeaked in panic.

"I'll be right back," he said gently, one paw against the glass. "But I've got to talk to the others." Jumping to the ground, he trotted toward the cats hidden amongst the honeysuckle. "The bird says Pris is in a trap that's been pushed into a creek."

"Creek?" Zekki jumped to his feet. "What creek?"

"Out past the pecan grove. Across the highway."

The white cat shrank back. "Highway?"

"Yes," Buddy said. "I can't leave till I figure a way to get Shan Dara out. So it's up to you. The bird will take you there."

"Across the highway?" Zekki repeated dully. "Alone?"

Buddy rubbed against the white cat's shoulder. "Don't worry. I won't be long. There're some broken panes in the window we might be able to push out."

"I'll go with you," Soot said, limping from the shadows.

Zekki drew a deep breath. "No, no, you've done enough, and besides, you're hurt."

"I feel better today. I can do it. I want to."

"But what about the old woman?" Buddy said, watching closely. "You just found a home; do you want to take the chance of losing it?"

Soot's head was high. "She loves me. She'll be here when I get back."

Buddy nodded, eyes bright with approval. "Then you both need to hurry. Pris is injured, and there's a snake."

"Snake?" a voice said from behind the bushes.

The animals twirled in surprise as the possum ambled through the brush and into the clearing. He stretched and yawned. "I love snakes."

Soot stared in amazement. "But we thought you were dead!"

The possum furrowed his brow. "No," he finally said, scratching one black ear and looking confused. "I don't think I've ever actually been dead."

"You were!" the black cat insisted. "We all saw you!"

"Okay, this is how it goes." The possum took a deep breath. "I get scared. I fall asleep. I wake up." He shrugged. "Then I usually eat something."

"But are you hurt?" Zekki crept closer, sniffing the animal's tail, which was cut and swollen.

Snapping it over his head, the possum winced. "Nope, I don't think so. Just a little sore." He glanced at the body of the chow with indifference. "So, where's the snake?"

"Across the highway," Buddy said. "The bird will show you."

"Let's go then. I'm starving."

"Wait a minute." Zekki stared at the ground. "I just . . . " he swallowed. "What I'm trying to say is that I'm really sorry I got us all into this. Buddy told me the Outs were dangerous. He tried to tell me a lot of things, but I was mad and dumb and wouldn't listen and—"

"You listened to yourself," Buddy said gently. "Sometimes it's the only voice that matters." He turned to include Soot. "I'll meet you as soon as I get Shan Dara out of the shed. Be careful. Jett's waiting, and I don't have to tell you what he's capable of."

"We know," Soot answered, crooked tail held high.

"We won't let you down."

Buddy watched them move toward the highway, the cats in the lead, the possum ambling behind, while above them the bird flew in widening circles, a specter of vengeance against the harsh August sky.

TWENTY-EIGHT

ZEKKI STOOD A SAFE DISTANCE from the highway, staring at the pecan grove on the other side. The trees stood in pristine rows, leaves rippling like emerald waves against hazy clouds.

Behind the winding plank fence, he pictured branches heavy with pecans, their lush harvest a tangle of shadows on the grass, and he longed to be there, hidden by their cool protection.

In contrast, the two-lane blacktop stretched to the west, its inky surface signaling treachery and death. With a shudder Zekki eyed the buckled pavement. Although it was still morning, heat already rose in a shimmering haze from its grimy face. By noon tiny pockets of tar would ooze between the crevices, a scorching trap for unprotected paws. It was plain the animals had to cross now, but the stench of gasoline, gravel, and grease made Zekki's stomach roll, and the memory of Soot's blood on the curb left him too frightened to move.

"What are you waiting for?" the mockingbird called, swooping toward him.

Her wings fluttered close to Zekki's head, and he flinched. "Are you sure there's no other way to the pecan grove?"

She landed boldly on the ground, her face pinched with irritation. "If you can fly. But since I've never seen any of you do that, the answer is no."

Soot limped through the weeds and eased himself onto the grass. His leg was still swollen, and he gingerly licked an angry red welt before scanning the highway. "Why've you stopped? Aren't we going?"

Zekki looked away. "I can't believe you're willing to cross this thing again."

"It's not like I'm looking forward to it."

"But you're ready to do it. What's wrong with me? I'm not the one who was hurt."

"There's nothing wrong with you," Soot said gently. "All good things are afraid of evil."

Zekki studied the skinny black cat before him, unmindful of the midmorning sun growing steadily hotter, its merciless glare beating down on his back. Even in the glare of sunlight, Soot's fur looked matted and dull. The wounded leg bent unnaturally at the joint, suggesting permanent damage, and his posture was continuously fearful and wary. Yet for all that, he radiated a stalwart commitment to honor and an under-stated courage that could be counted on. Soot was definitely Buddy's son, and looking into those familiar golden eyes, Zekki wondered why he'd never made the connection before.

"What's going on?" The possum pushed between them, eyeing the mockingbird with friendly interest. "Have the plans changed or something?"

"Yes," the bird muttered impatiently. "We're waiting for the cats to levitate."

Soot gave Zekki a nod of encouragement, then hobbled toward the curb. "No, nothing's changed, we're just making sure there're no cars coming."

The possum glanced at the road, started to speak, then stopped, mesmerized by something in the far lane. "Bug," he said, his voice low and trancelike. "Breakfast bug." He lurched onto the pavement, his nose down, his beady eyes riveted to the hapless insect who now scrambled frantically across the white stripe.

Zekki watched in horror. "What are you doing?"

A muffled roar of engines vibrated in the stillness, and Soot looked alarmed. "He shouldn't be out there now."

The possum ambled further into the street, his focus unwavering.

"Stop!" Zekki screamed, his voice shrill and hysterical.

"If he's going across, he should do it fast!" the mocking-bird shrieked from above them. "Cars are coming!"

Tires rumbled in the distance; sun glinted off metal.

Soot scrambled off the curb. "Forget the food. Run!"

Oblivious to the commotion, the possum snatched the insect with one black paw and popped it in his mouth. A horn blared from behind, and he looked up in surprise, then terror. Eyes rolling back, his body sagged.

The cats watched, rigid with fear.

"Don't do that again!" Zekki ran helplessly along the curb. "Wake up!"

The first car braked hard as a truck slammed into its rear

bumper. Skidding sideways, they slid in a lazy circle before screeching to a stop three feet from the possum, who toppled onto the asphalt, his mouth alive with six writhing legs still thrashing in protest.

Without thinking, Zekki bolted onto the asphalt. Dodging broken glass and a taillight that had just crashed to the ground, he grabbed the creature by the scruff of his neck, pulling him into a sitting position. "Get up! Now isn't the time to be dead!"

The bitter stench of burning rubber filled the air, and angry drivers piled into the street where they pointed and screamed, furiously pushing numbers on cell phones.

Shaking his head in confusion, the possum swallowed the beetle in one easy gulp and hiccupped. "What's going on?"

Soot darted between them. "We've gotta get out of here!"

Nudging the possum to his feet, the animals streaked across the highway, past steaming vehicles and gesticulating drivers, and leaped over the curb to safety. Sides heaving, they crouched in the grass, staring at the commotion they'd created.

Traffic had come to a grinding halt, and sirens wailed in the distance.

"Are you crazy?" Zekki bawled, his fur bristling around his face, his eyes wild with anger. "You were almost killed out there!"

"Killed?" The possum's voice was bewildered and hurt. "When was I killed?"

"Out there!" the bird screeched. "You fell over in the highway! What's wrong with you?"

The possum looked from one animal to another. "Nothing's wrong with me." He shifted uneasily. "What's everybody staring at?"

In the street two men argued loudly, their shiny new SUVs piled against a U-Haul trailer whose dented side read: NEW MEXICO: LAND OF ENCHANTMENT. The driver leaped from his cab, the altercation erupting into blows.

Turning with interest, the possum's eyes shifted from the fight to a white sack that had fallen from the front seat of a battered car. "Whoa, are those donuts?" he said, staggering toward the curb.

"No!" both cats wailed in unison.

The possum stopped, shaking his head with frustration. "What's wrong with everybody? I'm normally asleep by now; if you don't want me to come with you, that's okay but just tell me, because otherwise I'm gonna go back, eat something closer to the dumpster, and turn in."

"It's not like that." Soot moved to the creature's side and touched his nose. "We want you to come, but you need to be careful."

"I am careful." His black eyes were friendly and brimming with goodwill. He squinted at the sky. "Lunch time!" he called, trotting gaily toward the grove, back arched, tail high.

"You did it," Soot said softly to Zekki. "You crossed the highway and saved his life."

Zekki turned in surprise. It was true. The dreaded asphalt lay behind him, crowded with angry people and wrecked machinery, but there were no dead animals. The white cat's heart beat with new confidence, and he turned toward the black cat with appreciation. "I didn't do it alone."

Dipping his head in shy acknowledgment, Soot skittered ahead. "Come on, Pris is waiting."

And Jett, thought Zekki, following his friend until their shadows entwined. *And Jett.*

The Animal Control van pitched and jiggled over potholes as the street progressed into a drab and ill-kempt neighborhood. Judy hummed along with the radio, arm draped out the open window, towering French twist protected by a shiny purple nylon scarf tied carefully beneath her chin. Humming louder, she turned up the volume.

Curt scowled and switched the music off. "Okay. We're on Sixth, and we're really close to Willing," he said to the dispatcher. "Where did she say the dogs were?" He listened intently. "Got it." Clicking off the phone, he turned to Judy. "Somebody called this morning; said they heard dogs fighting last night, and now there's a dead one behind their house. Could be our boy."

"Hmmm." Judy turned the rearview mirror and applied a shimmering coat of lip gloss that filled the cab with a gagging sweetness.

"Hey!" Curt twisted the mirror to its original position. "I've asked you not to fool with that."

Undaunted, she flipped it back and inspected her teeth. "What's the matter, afraid the chow's already dead and you won't get to kill it?"

Curt narrowed his eyes, then turned right at a stop sign.

"Here's the place," he announced, pulling the truck to the curb.

An obese young woman was sprawled on a lawn chair, slapping listlessly at mosquitoes. "Are you the animal guys?" she said, swigging from a bottle of Coke.

Curt nodded.

"Okay, the dog's back there by the tool shed. It'd probably be easier if you go through the alley, though. There's a gate in the fence. Just drive right on through; it ain't locked or nothin'."

"Thanks." Curt threw the gear in reverse and turned around.

The truck maneuvered carefully through the debris of the alley. A tool shed was clearly visible over the wisteria-draped fence, and Curt parked the vehicle as close to it as possible.

"Let's do this thing." Stuffing some gloves into his back pocket, he jumped out and headed through the gate.

Judy stole one last look in the visor mirror, then followed.

The stiffening body of a yellow dog lay propped against the door of the shed. Flies buzzed around its muzzle, clinging to the black blood drying in a sticky pool by its shoulders.

"You know what?" Curt said, squatting down and waving the insects away. "I'll bet you anything this is him." Pulling on gloves, he lifted its head. "Whoa, check this. Something just about ripped its throat out."

Judy stood up and looked around. Darkness beneath the bushes caught her attention, and she cautiously walked toward it. "Hey!" she called, moving closer. "Here's another one!"

A large German shepherd lay at her feet. There were no obvious injuries, but it appeared to be dead. She leaned down to look at its collar, and the dog twitched, drawing a barely perceptible breath. "Curt! This one's alive, and it belongs to somebody. I'm going to get the tags and call them from the truck." She started to undo the buckle, then screamed as a small shape darted from under the animal's head, scurried over her ankle, and fled into the bushes.

"What's going on?" Curt said, running to where she now stood hysterically brushing her legs.

"Get it off, get it off!" she squealed, spinning in a circle and stamping her feet. "Is something on me?"

"What are you talking about? I don't see anything."

Judy hugged herself. "I was looking at the dog, and something jumped on me."

Rolling his eyes, Curt knelt beside the shepherd, running a practiced hand across its body. "I don't see any wounds." He lifted the dog's lips, revealing pale gums and yellowed canines. "But she's definitely old and in bad shape." Standing up, he glanced at the chow. "Let's load 'em and get this one to a vet."

Judy waited by the shed while Curt carried the shepherd to the truck and placed her on a tarp in the back. Leaning against the rough wood, Judy relaxed in the morning sun, picking at some peeling paint and wishing they'd break for lunch, when something rattled inside the shed. Startled, she went to the grimy window, wiped it with her palm, and looked in.

Behind dirt-smeared glass, two periwinkle eyes stared in

wide surprise, then disappeared into the darkness amid a flurry of dust.

"Look at this!" she shouted. "There's a Siamese cat trapped in there! Aren't we looking for a Siamese?"

Curt trotted to where she stood, pressing his face against the casement. "Yeah, I see it under the bench." He slapped his thigh. "Awesome! First we find the dog and now this!"

"Maybe it belongs to somebody around here."

"Naw," he said, wiping off another pane for a better look. "Look at that fancy collar. I'd be surprised if anyone in this neighborhood owns a purebred like that. Bet you anything it's one of those cats." He ran to the front of the shed, pushed the chow to the side with his foot, and held the door shut. "Go get the snare."

Judy sprinted toward the truck, grabbed the pole, and ran back to Curt, who held out one muscular arm. "Just pass it to me easy now."

"You're not gonna believe this," Judy said quietly, "but look to your right."

Curt turned to see a yellow cat crouched by the shed, ears flat, eyes narrow and fixed. "Man, oh man," he said in a hoarse whisper. "We've got 'em both! We . . ." He stopped, brow creased with confusion. The cat didn't appear alarmed or sick; in fact, it was creeping forward, expression fierce, focused, and strangely intelligent.

"What are you waiting for?" Judy hissed. "Just snare him, and let's get this thing over with."

"I—I don't know," Curt stammered, instinctually moving back. "Something's wrong . . ."

The cat moved closer, tail still, whiskers quivering.

"He's—he's stalking you," Judy said, tugging his sleeve. "I think we should back off . . ."

With a guttural moan, the cat sprang upward, claws extended, spitting in fury.

"What the—" Curt shielded his head, tripped over the chow, and fell backward as the cat streaked passed, whirled in the dust, and approached again, muscles undulating in a smooth, confident movement. Curt scrambled for footing, his voice breaking with panic. "Get the snare! Get the snare!" Covering his face, he struggled to stand.

Judy started forward, then stopped, as the cat changed direction. "Oh, my God!" she screamed. "It's coming after me! Help! It's rabid! It's . . ." With a grunt she stumbled over the snare and fell in a tangle across Curt who had just risen to his knees.

"Get off me!" he shouted, lurching to his feet as the shed door creaked open. Helplessly, he watched the Siamese dart to freedom, the yellow tom bounding behind.

Judy sprawled by the chow, mouth gaping. "It got me! I—I was attacked! Did you see it?"

Brushing off his pants, Curt huffed with fury, hands shaking. "No, I didn't see it! I was too busy trying to keep my freakin' eyes from being clawed out!"

"But I tore my scarf and messed up my haaaaaair!" she wailed.

Curt checked himself for wounds and frowned, surprised to find none.

"I'm not going out again unless we have guns or something!" Judy screeched, voice rising with hysteria. "I want hazard pay!"

"Listen." Curt snarled, jerking her to her feet, their faces almost touching. "You're not hurt, and you're not going to say anything about this to anybody."

She sniffed, mouth puckered with indignation. "But— but we were—"

"You wanna lose your job? You wanna see this story in the newspaper?" He framed an imaginary headline with beefy hands. "ANIMAL CONTROL OFFICERS ATTACKED BY KITTY. WOMAN'S HAIR SCREWED UP." He stepped back. "Do you?"

Judy reluctantly shook her head.

"Okay, so here's our story." Curt paused and nervously licked his lips. "The cats were ripped to shreds by both those dogs before we ever got here, okay? We looked for their heads to bring back for testing, but something must've dragged 'em off during the night. Got it? I'm already up to here with the department, and they don't need to know I was—" he paused, voice rising with rage and humiliation "—that I was ambushed by some . . . some freak of freakin' nature! We got the chow, the cats are dead, end of story." He squinted for emphasis and leaned closer, squeezing her arm. "I'm not kidding, Judy. Keep your mouth shut!"

"Okay, okay!" She jerked away. "I heard you!" Flouncing toward the truck, she furiously straightened her shirt. "You don't even care about me!" she called. "I could've been *killed*!"

Curt followed, holding the snare out in front of him like a spear. "Stay away from me, you freakin' freak," he mumbled to the shadows, trickles of sweat rolling down his jaw. "I know you're out there. Jumping in the truck with Judy, Curt turned on the engine and roared down the alley, dust puffing like smoke beneath the wheels.

TWENTY-NINE

SHAFTS OF LIGHT STREAMED through the mesquite leaves, reflecting sunbeams off the water. Pris raised her head, squinting against the glare. Above her the white Texas sun blasted a searing preview of temperatures to come, and the creatures of the creek bustled with activity. Squirrels tumbled through branches in fearless acrobatics, while grackles the size of terriers strutted by the bank, their black feathers shining with incandescent blues and purples, their yellow eyes bright and clever.

The movement made Pris dizzy, and she lowered her head, calmed by the burble of water lapping around the cage. For a moment she felt relaxed, wanting to fall back against the glistening wire and sleep, but even in her disoriented state she knew that wasn't a good idea.

Something bad had happened, though the exact details were foggy. She remembered going into the cage for food, but where was she now? Her brow wrinkled, and a dark memory shoved its way to the surface. Jett! His voice permeated her brain, cruel and mocking. He had pushed her into the water, left her for dead! She opened her eyes wide. He was after Zekki and Buddy as well!

Waves rolling in moonlight, feathers beating the water.

There had been a mockingbird! And she had gone to get help! Tangles of details clamored for attention, but Pris's head ached, and the sun felt so good she yawned, welcoming a dream-filled escape. She jerked awake. There was something else, though, something even more terrible and frightening. She tried to remember, but thoughts flickered out of reach, dissolving in a drone of mosquitoes. With a deep, careful breath, she rolled to her stomach. Her ribs were sore, and an acrid taste of blood filled her mouth, but for the most part, she felt okay. Maybe she could even stand. Rising on trembling haunches, she took a wobbly step forward. The cage slid farther into the creek, its water covering her front paws in icy ripples. Startled, she tried to steady herself, but her muscles shook so violently she stumbled against the wire, and the trap tipped forward again, continuing its slow slide into the creek. "Help!" she called. "Somebody help me! I'm here!"

Behind her something dropped on the trap, its weight tipping the enclosure backward and stopping further movement.

The bird had brought help! With a whimper of gratitude, she turned awkwardly in the cage, words of thanks already forming . . . words that quickly turned to hisses of shock and fear.

Tongue flicking, head erect, the frightening "thing" she'd forgotten uncoiled four feet of muscle and glided silently toward the door.

The animals hurried through the pecan grove, their labored

breathing harsh in the shadowed silence. Rigid rows of trees formed a natural pathway to the golf course, and pecans in bright lime husks plopped to the ground.

Though filled with an increasing sense of urgency, Zekki knew that Soot was falling behind. Slowing to a trot, he stopped beneath a tree. "Why don't we take a little break? I think the bird said the golf course is beyond that stand of trees."

"Yeah." Soot's voice was faint and winded. "That would be good."

The possum flopped to his side without comment, and the cats settled down, their tongues cleaning debris from their coats and tails.

Above them the mockingbird skimmed through the branches, finally landing in a particularly large pecan tree. Hopping forward, she approached a camouflaged nest and peered into the twiggy structure. With a screech of anguish she shot skyward, bursting from the grove and looping in wild circles against the sapphire sky.

"Where's she going?" the possum asked, standing up and watching her small figure disappear from sight.

Soot gazed through the leafy canopy. "I don't know for sure, but I think her mate was killed here." He nodded toward the ground, and they turned, eyes fixed on a spray of taupe feathers scattered in the leaves.

Zekki's mouth watered at the sight, and ashamed, he jumped to his feet. "We need to keep moving. She'll be back."

Both the possum and Soot had difficulty keeping up with Zekki, who darted beneath a fence, charged fearlessly across a road, and ran onto the rolling fairways.

As predicted, the mockingbird reappeared without explanation, her demeanor subdued but committed, and directed them as they ran. "The creek is right beyond those houses to the right!" Flitting close to their heads, she swooped upward. "Follow me!"

Dodging sand traps and sprinkler heads, the little group slunk behind bushes, waiting impatiently as golfers played the course, their carts eventually disappearing up an immaculate green. After a brief pause for water and some backtracking for safety, the cats and possum raced behind the mockingbird's darting shadow, eventually skidding to a stop at the backyard of a towering two-story home.

"She's down that ravine." The bird flew further into the yard and past some trees. "Be careful, though; it's a jagged drop with a creek at the bottom."

Soot and Zekki crouched low to the ground, bellies dragging through trailing vines of ivy and jasmine.

Behind them the possum scurried in the underbrush, preferring to keep as close to the sprawling foliage as possible.

"I'm going down to get a closer look." With a tilt of her wings, the bird soared over the ravine, disappearing into the trees below.

The trio crept to the edge of the cliff and looked down. Beneath them the creek wound in a glittering ribbon of water. Mud and gravel covered the banks, leading to a precipice of jutting rocks and weeds.

"She's there! In the trap! I see her!" Zekki whispered, his voice hoarse with excitement.

Pris's plump form was vaguely visible through the mesh. She hissed loudly, her face inches from a blob of darkness coiled by the door.

The possum leaned over, whiskers forward, nose wiggling. "And the snake. It's a big one, too." Stretching his back legs, he snapped his tail and did some calisthenic-type hops and lunges. "Okay, I'm ready." He turned to the cats. "I'll call you when I'm through."

Zekki wrinkled his forehead, bewildered. "When you're through? I thought we were all going."

"Nope, just me."

"Why? We know what's down there. We're not afraid."

The possum sniffed at a nettle, then casually scratched his ear. "Have you ever actually seen a snake before?"

"Yes, well, no . . ."

"Ever kill one?"

Both cats exchanged glances and shook their heads.

"That's why I'm saying you shouldn't go down there," the possum said, his earnest face solemn and set. "And don't let Pris know we're here, either. Not yet."

"I didn't come all this way to do nothing!" Zekki's voice rose with frustration.

"But you've already done your part," the possum said.

Frowning, Zekki narrowed his eyes. "What are you talking about? I haven't done anything."

"You got us here, didn't you?"

"But—but this is different," Zekki stammered. "I mean, we're a team, and I don't think you should go alone."

"Have to. It won't work if I don't." The possum

shrugged, heading for the cliff. "I've already talked to the bird. We have a plan, and she knows what to do." He looked at their doubtful faces. "Trust me. Snakes are my specialty." Before they could protest, he scrambled over the rocky edge and began the steep descent toward the water.

The cats watched him slip against a boulder, regain his balance, then traverse sideways across the ragged terrain. With one last look, he flicked his tail in salute, then disappeared behind a rock formation.

"What if he doesn't kill it?" Zekki said. "What if it kills him? You saw what he did at the highway, maybe he's all talk, maybe he—"

"Don't underestimate the possum," Soot interrupted. "He's a wild thing, and wild things have their ways."

The water moccasin tightened his coil and watched the cat closely. She looked bigger now that she was on her feet.

Flattening her ears, the cat moaned a low, guttural warning.

The snake wasn't concerned. He had studied every inch of the cage during the night, and he knew exactly how to get in; but getting in wasn't the goal. The goal had been to wait for the mockingbird to come back so he could kill and eat her . . . and she had, only instead of hovering around the cage like before, she was sitting in a tree, watching him. Lifting his head, he glared at the bird staring impudently from a low-hanging branch. He bumped the cage with frustration. The bird had been right there in the water, so close he could have touched her, and then the loud-mouthed cat had warned her and ruined everything. He peered through the wire with malice. Hunger was clouding his judgment, and he considered sliding into the cage, killing her, and forgetting about the bird all together.

Sensing a vibration from behind, he swiveled his head for a better look. The bank was empty and still—too still. Something wasn't right. Uncoiling from the metal door, he undulated toward the safety of the bushes.

Fluttering from her perch, the bird landed on the ground beneath the oak.

The snake watched, stunned. She was almost within striking distance. Cautiously, he changed direction, his tail quivering with aggression.

Cocking her head, the bird hopped a little closer, ignoring him and preening her feathers.

He inched forward until he could see the fine gray quills around her beak, then stopped. Unbelievably, she appeared not to notice, and he slid toward her once more, this time, a third of his body raised, preparing to strike.

Branches rustled above, and before he could move, something fell from the tree, its weight dragging him backward. Thrashing in the mud, the snake writhed and twisted in desperation, mouth gaping in silent fury as the possum clung to its head, razor teeth grinding steadily through muscle and bone.

"He has him!" the mockingbird screamed, soaring over the cats who watched transfixed from the cliff.

With one last contortion, the snake arced his spine, then flopped limply to one side, his head partially severed, his tongue twitching between slack jaws.

The possum sat in the mud, a chunk of flesh caught in his teeth and his whiskers red with blood. "Piece of cake." Panting, he licked his chops. "Hey!" he called to the cats, now tumbling down the embankment and running toward the cage. "Are you gonna eat this?"

Zekki tripped on a limb, rolling sideways into a crevice. Brambles tore at his ears and clumps of mud clung to his fur, but he didn't care. "Pris!" he howled. "Pris!"

The calico stumbled weakly to the end of the trap. At first she didn't have the strength to squirm through the narrow opening, but finally she managed, and collapsed with exhaustion on the bank. Zekki fell beside her, his dirty paws entwined in her fur. Their sobs of joy mingled with throaty purrs of comfort and moans of distress.

"I knew you'd come," she whimpered, burying her head in his matted coat. "I knew you would."

THIRTY

THE CREEK RANG WITH JOYOUS LAUGHTER, and Soot stood back from the water, suddenly awkward and embarrassed in the face of such emotion. He watched Zekki and Pris join the possum and mockingbird beneath the mesquite. They shared the snake, congratulating one another as comrades, while Soot stood alone, the uninvited guest at a party he'd helped to plan.

A familiar loneliness engulfed him. He had always been an outsider, even in the alley, and memories of life on the sidelines squeezed his heart with a familiar ache.

His mouth quivered with self-pity. He'd left the old woman; jeopardized his only chance for happiness and for what? They hadn't even missed him. Limping toward the cliffs, the sun stung his back. With luck he could make his way to the highway by late afternoon; maybe even be at the house by dark. Searching for a solid toehold amid the smooth rocks and sifting dirt, he clamored upward.

"I could have told you they would never accept you," a smooth voice said.

Above him Jett stood on a rocky ledge, his great paws flexing, his head tilted with amusement.

Soot crouched to the ground, torn between running for cover and begging for mercy. "That's not true. They're my friends," he mumbled, feeling doubly betrayed and vulnerable.

The big tom leaned closer, his eyeless socket oozing a thick, wet rivulet down his face. "Really?" He nodded toward the mesquite, where the animals now stretched in companionable silence, their bellies bulging and content. "Then why aren't you reveling in the grand celebration?"

"I'm not hungry."

"You're lying."

Soot sagged, ashamed by the truth.

"You risked your life for those ingrates, and now that they have what they want, you're forgotten." Jett moved to another rock with serpentine stealth. "To them you're just a pathetic cripple from the alley; sometimes useful, but not really wanted. They'll never appreciate you"—he paused— "like I do."

Soot shrank back, frightened and confused. "But you hate me."

"Hate you?" Jett blinked, his broad face earnest and hurt. "How could I hate you? You're family to me."

It was true. Soot couldn't remember a time when Jett hadn't been in his life. He wondered how he could have forgotten that and felt a wrench of guilt followed by waves of apprehension. What was Jett trying to tell him? A familiar fear tightened his chest. Was it something he'd suspected since kittenhood, but was too afraid to ask?

"Come back home." Jett's voice was low and intense.

"Come back to the alley, the place where you were born, where you're understood . . . where your mother died."

"My mother?" Soot remembered Ahn-ya's sweet face, and his throat ached with longing for her soft fur and gentle ways.

Ahn-ya. The thought was suddenly disturbing. Ahn-ya and Jett . . . always together.

You're family to me.

"We had many conversations about her pride in you," Jett continued. "She knew you were exceptional, just as I do." He watched Soot, his eye boring into him. "Do you know why I'm telling you this?"

Soot tried to swallow the shameful words waiting to be said, but it was no use. "Yes." He squared his shoulders, preparing for the worse. "It's because . . . you're my father, aren't you?"

The big cat seemed startled, then recovered his composure, his one eye slit and cunning. "Why, yes, Soot, that's exactly right," he finally said, words carefully chosen. "I'm . . . your . . . father. I was going to tell you . . . later, but you've guessed the truth, and I think Ahn-ya would want it this way."

Bile rose in Soot's throat. So it was finally out in the open. The thing he had secretly feared the most. He was Jett's son. Tears of humiliation filled his eyes. He thought of his friends by the creek and sighed with a new understanding. They'd probably known all along. Maybe they'd even felt sorry for him, but they'd never really trusted him. Soot smiled bitterly. Who would? He stared at the big cat with resignation. "Why are you telling me this now?"

Jett stood, his jagged shadow crawling dark and oppressive

over the black cat's face. "Because there's a change coming, Soot. Changes that will make them regret their arrogance and disrespect . . . something that will bring us greatness and Ahn-ya honor." He leaned forward, his eye shining with emotion. "And you can be a part of it . . . my second in command, my most cherished confidant and advisor." He paused for emphasis. "My *son*."

Soot winced and tried to hide it with a shrug. "What change?"

Swiveling his head, Jett looked directly into the black cat's eyes. "I'm afraid I could only entrust that information to someone of whose loyalty I was certain. The kind of loyalty I had from your mother, for instance." His ears moved forward. "Have I your loyalty, Soot? Will you take up your mother's cause . . . and mine?"

Soot heard Zekki and Pris laughing with the possum in the distance. They had probably eaten everything, hadn't even looked for him or wondered where he was or if he was hungry. The scent of blood still hung in the air, and his stomach growled and churned. "But how can I help?"

"Well, let's see." Jett's massive body stiffened, and only the tip of his thick tail twitched. "Perhaps you have some information that might be useful . . . about Buddy, for instance?" He leaned forward, his voice harsh and strained. "He's the enemy of the alley, you know, dangerous and not to be trusted!"

"Buddy," Soot repeated, rising to his feet and moving slowly toward the rocks.

The sounds of his companions faded in the distance, and

his mind was consumed with the great, glowing eye beckoning from the shadows.

He remembered Ahn-ya.

He wouldn't let her down.

THIRTY-ONE

BUDDY STOOD BENEATH A PECAN TREE sniffing the air.
Mother had been generous. A mélange of scents, wild and
musky, swirled through the orchard, and he lowered his head
with satisfaction. Everyone was accounted for, from the pungent smell of the possum to the dusty tang of the bird.

Shan Dara lay beside him, her sides heaving from the
stress of the highway and the midmorning heat. Already
thin, her flanks seemed alarmingly sunken, and he realized
she hadn't really eaten for two days. "I'm sorry I've had to
push you so hard." He licked the top of her creamy head. "I
know you're tired."

"No, it's all right." She looked up and yawned. "But I'm
so sleepy. Couldn't we take a break? It doesn't feel like I've
slept at all in the last few days." The lids of her periwinkle eyes
drooped with exhaustion. "Not a long rest, just a little one."

Buddy considered the request. It was important to find
Pris, but he also realized he couldn't push Shan Dara much
farther. The mingled aroma of the animals was faint, which

meant they had been here much earlier, but it was still strong enough to follow without much trouble. Carefully, he assessed the area. Sunlight flashed between heavy foliage, and swaying branches cast writhing patterns across the grass. Soon the grove would be washed in the mauve of evening, and it was imperative that they be at The Gathering by nightfall. That didn't give them much time.

The Siamese rustled beside him, and he looked with wonderment at her graceful body, stretched like alabaster in the shade. Her eyes were closed, and she had drifted into a deep sleep, her perfectly formed paws and tail twitching in fretful dreams.

Buddy leaned down, gently nudging her with his head. "Shan Dara?"

She stirred and looked up.

"I'm going to scout around a little and get a better idea of how to get to the creek. I want you to rest, but not in the open like this." A sprawling clump of lantana, golden blossoms just beginning to fade, caught his eye. "Why don't you crawl under there and get some more sleep? I'll be back soon."

With a groggy nod, she struggled to her feet. "Don't be gone long, though," she said, sliding under the prickly leaves. "You won't, will you?"

"No, just a quick look around is all. I don't expect any trouble, but if something should happen, anything at all, scream as loudly as you can, and I'll be right back. Okay?"

A blue eye peered anxiously between the saffron petals. "Okay, but be careful."

"I will." He turned to leave.

"Buddy?"

Her voice rang with emotion, and he stopped, vaguely alarmed.

"I need—I mean, I want to talk to you about something before you go." Pushing through the lantana, her face was serious. "Do you remember telling me that Indoors and Ferals weren't allowed to be together? That it was The Law?"

He nodded slowly.

She licked her chops with uncertainty. "What if a cat is born an Indoor, and then finds she doesn't want to be one anymore? What if . . ." she stared at the ground. "I mean, what if she wants to be a Feral, live in the Outs and be with . . . you know" she peeked at him shyly, "other Ferals?"

The question hung between them, fragile as a bubble, heavy as stone.

His mind spun. There was so much she didn't know, so much he couldn't tell her, and at the same time his heart thudded with a joy that was almost painful.

Her brow knotted with concentration. She watched him attentively, delicate whiskers fanning forward and trembling.

He started to speak, then stopped. Clearing his throat, he prayed for the right words and tried again. "Shan Dara, your people are probably looking for you right now. You've seen how things are in the Outs. Food and water are scarce, summers are hot, and they're nothing compared to winters. Right now this could be considered an adventure, but later, once you've been here for a while, you might wish you'd never seen me. Danger is everywhere, and I can't guarantee you'll be safe or—"

"I don't want guarantees," she interrupted quietly. "I just want you."

Squirrels quarreled in the treetops, their boisterous activity showering the cats with leaves and pecans. Oblivious of the war above them, the two cats stared at one another, barely breathing, their bodies tense.

"Please understand that once you take the vow, there's no turning back." He swallowed and shifted. "Are you sure?"

"Buddy," she said gently. "I understand the difference between adventure and commitment. I'm more than sure."

He blinked, not knowing whether to yowl with happiness or continue to discourage her.

"Believe me," she said, as though reading his mind. "I know what I'm doing. I just don't know *how* to do it."

"Well." He took a deep breath. "The Law says you must renounce the Indoors and all that it was and is and claim the Outs as your home forever."

"Is that what you did?"

The question caught him off guard, and he frowned. "What do you mean?"

"You said you thought if you could be an Indoor, all your worries would go away. So"—she cocked her head—"when you lived with The Boy, did you renounce the Outs?"

"Of course not!" he said vehemently. "I would never do that! I'm proud to be a Feral and would give my life to protect and serve my species."

"Then, don't you see?" Her face shone with tenderness. "You didn't abandon your own kind. Whatever your fears, whatever your doubts, you always intended to come back. This proves it."

The truth of her words engulfed him, and for the first time since the rescue, his life again had meaning. He blinked as though suddenly seeing light after years lived in darkness. The world was changed. Trees still towered, shadows played in sunlight, and the earth beneath his paws was cool and dry. But his future, no longer dim with uncertainty, shone before him, an oasis of clarity in periwinkle blue.

"Are you all right?" the Siamese asked.

Purrs of wonderment filled the air, and Buddy laughed with an ease he hadn't felt in years. "Yes, I'm all right! I'm more all right than I've ever been in my life!" He grew serious, watching her face intently. "I love you, Shan Dara, and if you still want to be with me, it would be an honor to walk with you always."

"And I love you." Coyly, she ducked her head. "And, of course, I still want to come with you." Taking a long, deep breath, she stood. "I'm ready, and I understand the words I'm to say, but"—her face scrunched with confusion—"now, I don't know who to say them to."

A familiar breeze ruffled their fur.

"The Wind," Buddy said. "She's our Mother, Guardian of The Feral and protector of all animals. She hears and knows everything we do."

With a nod of understanding, Shan Dara stepped into the clearing, her exquisite head tilted upward, her fine coat aglow in the filtered sun. "I, Shan Dara, leave the Indoor life that was mine." Her voice was clear and steady. "I say good-bye to the humans who loved me and go with gratitude." Turning, she blinked at Buddy, her gaze bright with tears. "On this day, I claim the Outs as my home, to live as one among The Feral and to embrace them as family and ally all the days of my life." She moved forward until her nose almost touched his. "Beneath the sacred Wind that guides us, I swear my intent."

A swirl of air, strangely cool for August, danced between them, blowing tiny yellow petals around their heads. In the distance, traffic churned and children played, but in the orchard there was only the quiet of contentment, blessed by The Wind.

A monotonous tapping pushed its way into Zekki's dreams. He and The Boy were running up an ebony highway, bright orange flames licking their heels. Then the landscape shifted, and The Boy was pushing him into a box, nailing it shut with a mallet that suddenly morphed into a handful of bright red geraniums. "You'll be safe here," The Boy panted, scarlet blooms dropping like blood through the narrowing crack. "We'll all be safe in the box."

Zekki awoke with a start, his blue eyes blinking in the mellow afternoon light, while above, a woodpecker clung to the mesquite, pecking a knothole with ferocity. The darkness of the dream quickly faded into the warmth of Pris's fragrant fur, and he snuggled closer to her sleeping form. Was it possible she was right here beside him, safe and unharmed? He sighed and stretched, enjoying the waning patch of sunlight and remembering the snake. Delicious. Soot had been right about the possum. A trickle of unease rolled through his mind, and he frowned. What about Soot? Raising his head, he looked around. The possum was curled up inside a rotting log, with only his tail showing, and the mockingbird dozed in an oak, head buried beneath her wing.

Where was Soot?

Leaping to his feet, Zekki sprinted toward the creek, his eyes wide with alarm. "Pris!" he called. "Have you seen Soot?"

Pris sat up, her face puzzled. "Soot was with you."

Desperately, Zekki ran near the embankment. "Soot! Soot!"

The possum opened one eye and yawned. "What's going on?"

"It's Soot! Zekki can't find Soot; have you seen him?"

The white cat dashed back to the group, his pink nose flushed with exertion. "He was right behind me when we ran down to the water."

Fluttering to the ground, the mockingbird shook her head. "I thought you knew where he was . . . you don't?"

"No! I don't remember seeing him after we found Pris!" Zekki's voice rose with hysteria. "We've got to find him!"

"Please don't yell," Pris begged, scurrying behind him. "Jett will hear you."

The possum crept from the log. "Wait a minute. I saw him."

They all listened, eyes desperate with hope.

"He was standing by the water, and then he turned and headed up the cliff again. I thought he was . . ." The possum stopped, scratching his head. "I don't know what I thought."

He brightened. "Hey, his leg isn't healed; maybe he needed to rest or something. I'll bet that's it—he's resting." There was false cheer in his voice, and the animals looked at one another in guilty silence.

"I'm going to find him," Zekki said quietly.

"But you can't go alone." Pris's soft paw strained to stop him.

"Stay together until I come back or Buddy shows up." With a determined nod, Zekki galloped along the creek, his pads slipping on wet stones, unmindful of the lapping water sloshing toward the bank. "Soot!" his voice rang through the clearing. "Soot! Answer me! Soooot!"

"Shan Dara?"

The Siamese stretched and groaned with pleasure. The orchard was shadowed and cool, and the sharp scent of lantana pierced through her sleep. Had someone been calling her name? Raising her head, she listened. A blue jay screeched in the distance, and she could hear the faraway swish of cars on the highway, but that was all. Buddy would be back soon, and it felt good to relax. She sighed, curling into a tighter ball.

"Shan Dara!" The voice was insistent, slightly harsh.

This was real! She rose to a crouch and peeked through the tangled stalks of foliage.

A dark figure moved toward her, and startled, she screamed.

THIRTY-TWO

BUDDY HURRIED ACROSS THE GOLF COURSE, its closely cropped grass like velvet against his pads. The possum's smell was so strong, he hardly needed to rely on anything else, but he could also detect Zekki and Soot's scents as well.

The lawn gave way to sand, then continued past paths and fountains, finally ending behind an imposing brick club-house. Buddy stopped, his eyes riveted on three dumpsters. Like hungry giants, they hunkered beneath a stand of junipers, their gaping mouths huge and open. Buddy fought for air, sickened by the wave of memories that seemed to engulf him.

It was another summer day, much like this one, and he and his brother had wandered too far from the alley. At first they played on the golf course as always, roughhousing in the sand, hunting by the pond, and kicking and biting in mock battle. But suddenly the play turned rough, and Buddy found himself fighting for real, fighting for his life. "Hey!" he shouted, break-ing loose from the larger cat's viselike grip and catapulting onto the rim of the dumpster. Its heavy lid was propped up with a pole, and Buddy balanced on the hot metal, sure that his adversary wouldn't follow. He was wrong. Jett leaped behind him, threatening to knock him into the dumpster's gaping hole. "What's the matter with you?" Buddy panted, teetering on the burning ridge, but the gray tabby advanced closer, his teeth exposed, his ears flat and close to his head.

"You have everyone fooled." Jett's voice was pinched with hate. "They don't know how you've tried to destroy me . . . how you've stolen everything that was mine."

"Huh?" Blinking with confusion, Buddy raised one paw in a futile warning.

The gray tom crept forward, his eyes slit with fury. "Buddy's so perfect," he mimicked. "Buddy's so smart."

"Wait . . ." Buddy said, inching away. "What are you doing?"

Jett gave a humorless grin. "I'm taking my life back, brother." With a howl, he leaped upward, powerful jaws opened wide.

Buddy rose to meet the attack, nails extended. He meant only to defend himself, maybe scratch an ear or nose and then escape, but instead, his claw snagged Jett's eye, sinking deeply into its liquid orb before he pulled it out, bloody and wet.

Screaming in agony, his brother knocked him into the dumpster, then slammed against the pole, which fell away as the gray tom jumped to safety. From outside the enclosure Jett howled with pain and fury. "Who's the smart one now?"

Finally there was only silence and a suffocating heat that rolled like lava through Buddy's nose and lungs. He didn't know how long he thrashed in the darkness shouting for help before he collapsed. Barely conscious, he heard the lid being lifted, and a boy's voice murmuring encouragement. The last thing he remembered were gentle hands laying him on the cool grass and stroking his fur.

He had never been back to this place . . . never wanted to come back. Even now he remembered his feelings of helplessness and smelled the rotting filth of that burning prison. A rustling of leaves jerked him into the present, and he whirled, teeth exposed.

"Buddy!" Zekki shouted, running toward him. The white cat's coat hung from his body in long, damp tangles, and burrs dotted his tail. There was something ominous about his appearance, and Buddy instinctively recoiled. "Did you find Pris?"

"Yes, she's fine. The possum killed the snake."

"Then what?"

Zekki exhaled, trying to catch his breath. "It's Soot. He's . . . he's gone."

A warning buzzed in Buddy's ears. "What do you mean, gone?"

"I mean he was with me until I found Pris, and then things happened fast, and I was so happy, and then we ate, and I guess we slept for a while." He paused, grimacing with frustration. "I didn't realize what had happened until I woke up. It's my fault. I've been up and down the creek bed all the way to the embankment. I can smell him, but I can't find him. He's just . . . gone."

"Any other scents?" But Buddy already knew the answer.

"Yes." The white cat's face contorted in misery. "Jett's. I don't know how long he was up there, but it's fresh."

Shutting his eyes, Buddy heard the angry words from that summer long ago.

Who's the smart one now?

He felt dizzy. Zekki was talking, only his voice seemed distorted and far away.

"Go back to the others," Buddy mumbled. "Ask the mockingbird to fly over the golf course and look for Soot. I'll meet you back by the creek."

Zekki's concerned face swam before his eyes, but finally the white cat reluctantly nodded and trotted away.

The sun spun toward the horizon, and a vision of Ahn-ya's delicate face appeared in Buddy's mind. He knew he wasn't dreaming, yet he clearly saw her standing in the pecan orchard, pawing the ground. His consciousness slid toward her pushing for answers, straining to understand.

She looked up, her green eyes wide, then stepped aside as a glow of light illuminated the shadowy pile at her feet. It was a clump of lantana, trampled stems bent backward, bright yellow flowers crushed and scattered.

Shan Dara was gone!

He tried to speak, but Ahn-ya shook her head as if to stop him. *It's time,* her thoughts whispered.

"Time for what?"

You know . . . You know . . .

Tenba's words slid through his mind, twisting and turning in a painful swirl of confusion.

He's dead . . . The Cat Master . . . his successor . . . who?

Buddy's brain felt hot and dry as though it might explode into cinders. He wanted to blot out Ahn-ya's face, shake himself back to the present, but the memories were like living things now, squirming and pushing their way to be heard.

Of all my blood . . . of all my blood . . . rise from the alley. Rise . . .

Ahn-ya's fading form floated closer. *Remember the dream,* she urged. *Remember it . . .* NOW!

The words burst through his mind like a volcano, crystal clear and unmistakable. *Rise from the alley!* they echoed. *Of all my blood, you are The Chosen!*

An icy silence descended, its cool nothingness a balm for his racing heart and shaking legs. Slowly he absorbed the words and their meaning. "It's me. I'm the one," he whispered. "The Cat Master was speaking to *me*." He closed his eyes, searching his mind for Ahn-ya, but her image had vanished and another one appeared. It was of an old black-and-white cat with pale blue eyes, eyes that had watched Buddy's every move on a spring day so long ago. "I remember you now, Father," he said to the already fading vision. "I understand who you were. I understand everything."

"I thought you might," a familiar voice said from behind him.

Buddy turned in slow motion, searching for the shadowy silhouette that watched defiantly from the top of a dumpster.

Jett gave a brisk nod of greeting. "Welcome home, brother." His eye narrowed. "I've been waiting for you."

Buddy approached the dumpster, surprised that its

232

looming form no longer frightened him. "You knew, didn't you? Those were your thoughts that broke the Master's connection. That's why you came back, why you never mentioned he was dead. You've known all along The Cat Master was my father—"

"*Our* father!" Jett interrupted, friendly demeanor gone. "And no, I didn't realize who He was until later. But I always remembered the first time I saw Him . . . and how He looked at you." Jett's voice shook. "And turned from me. I had to break the connection. You'd already poisoned The Master against me long ago. I was the one who should have been chosen. I've always been the one with the strength and courage and vision. But no! To Him, it was always you!" Jett took a breath. "But that's all going to change, brother. I've planned some lovely surprises for your long-awaited return."

"First things first," Buddy said quietly. "Where is Shan Dara?"

"Ask Soot. He's the one who took her."

A brisk wind rattled through the air, blowing sand and dirt around them.

"Soot would never do anything like that. Never!"

Hunkering against the increasing gusts, Jett's mouth stretched into a leering smile. "Of course he would. He did it for me and the future of our kind."

Buddy swallowed hard, a nasty premonition tugging at his brain. "What do you mean?"

"What I mean"—Jett's eye gleamed with malevolence—"is that I've been looking for a proper mate, now that Ahn-ya is gone, and I think Shan Dara will be perfect. She's extremely exotic." The big cat smirked. "And those blue eyes will make my lineage very distinctive."

"What have you done to her!" Buddy screamed, lunging toward the dumpster.

"Meet me tonight at The Gathering," Jett said, backing into the shadows. "And I'll show you."

With a yowl, Buddy sprang against the metal, his claws barely grazing Jett's flank as he leaped into the bushes. Mocking laughter floated on the wind and flurries of leaves blew across the dumpster's rusted lid.

Buddy stood in the fading sunlight, his muscles twitching and tense. The Gathering! The new Cat Master would be anointed tonight. His mind raced. Jett would do anything to stop Buddy's coronation, and if his plan succeeded, Zekki, Pris, and Shan Dara would be in great danger. The old Master's words echoed in Buddy's brain, and a resolute sense of duty filled his heart. He would honor his father's wishes . . . even if it cost him his life.

THIRTY-THREE

ORIE PUSHED THROUGH THE WEEDS, then stopped, checking the area for predators. He'd never been this far from the crawl space, and though his stomach ached from hunger and thirst burned his throat, the Animal Control Officer's words propelled him forward. Tenba was alive! Miraculously she'd survived the night, and hopefully her woman had been notified and was on the way to claim her.

Struggling over rocks and limbs, Orie rooted beneath a grimy sock where he lay quietly, his ears focused on every sound. Alleys were deceptively empty during the day, their silent corridors of rotting wood and ancient chain-link simply a refuge for brambles, vines, and rubbish. But nighttime was different. The smallest shadows sprang to life, all gaping jaws and razor teeth, and every noise held the promise of food, no matter how meager.

Scurrying from his hiding place, Orie ran close to the fence, veered under a patch of nettles, and stopped to catch his breath beneath their fuzzy leaves. He had been traveling

all day, and if he kept going—pushed on no matter what—
he should be back on Sixth Avenue before dawn.

The moon was full and high overhead, partially illuminating the darkness. Although the alley seemed empty, it was
unlikely that it was. Predators rarely announced themselves
until you were sliding down their throats, and the lizard
wasn't taking any chances. With one last look in each direction, he took two bold steps forward, then stopped in horror.

Crouched in the door of an abandoned doghouse, a rat
stretched its neck, vigorously sniffing the air.

To Orie's right a large dandelion splayed in the dust, and
diving for cover, he watched wide-eyed as a pebble rolled
lazily from beneath his foot.

The rat snapped its head toward the movement and narrowed its eyes.

"I was saved for great things. I'm special, I'm special,"
Orie chanted silently, peering in terror from behind one
claw.

Apparently the rat agreed, because it licked its chops and
moved in Orie's direction.

The mockingbird should have been back by now. Buddy
stood by the creek, scanning the star-spattered sky, his tail
twitching with agitation. Jett was insane. Their conversation
by the dumpsters confirmed it, and the knowledge left him
weary, depressed, and afraid. Not for himself—he was prepared to accept his own fate—but the lives of Shan Dara and
the others were another matter.

The possum was gone, foraging for food, and Pris and

Zekki sat in the shelter of the mesquite. They hadn't approached Buddy since his return from the golf course, but he could sense their unasked questions. "Don't worry," he said, trying to keep his tone casual. "The bird's just going to fly around . . . see what's going on. Everything's fine. When she gets back we'll—"

"Is it true what Zekki said?" Pris interrupted.

"I don't know." Buddy laughed without humor. "He says a lot of things."

"Is Jett really your brother?"

Cicadas yammered from a nearby thicket, and a frog plopped into the creek.

"Yes," Buddy said, watching the moon-splashed water. "He is."

They sat in strained silence.

"What's happened to Soot and Shan Dara?" Pris asked softly.

Buddy looked into her frightened face and felt a pang of grief. She was an Indoor, unprepared for what had happened. She should be curled in The Boy's lap, not cowering in the darkness, covered in mud. "Don't worry about Soot," Buddy said. "He's a Feral and understands the Outs." A sudden vision of Shan Dara flashed in his mind, and he turned away, too distraught to continue.

"I found something!" The mockingbird sailed across the ravine and over the creek. With a fluttering of wings, she landed in the mesquite, her breast heaving with exertion.

Buddy leaped onto the tree trunk, claws gripping the battered bark, eyes gleaming. "What?"

"Cats." Nervously, the bird moved to a higher branch. "On the golf course."

"I expected that. How many?"

"A lot."

"Jett?"

"He's there, too, and he's talking to them." The bird paused. "He's saying some pretty nasty things about you. And they're listening."

"It doesn't matter. Did you see Soot?"

"No."

He tried to keep his voice steady. "Shan Dara?"

"No." She ruffled her feathers with discomfort. "Sorry."

Buddy twisted to the ground, his face dark with worry. Had Soot really betrayed them? If not, then where was he? "It's not your fault," he said to the bird. "Thanks for the information." For a few moments, he paced in the clearing, trying to quiet his mind. Things were rapidly coming to a head. Once The Gathering was under way, it would be hard to stop whatever plans Jett had put into motion, and as much as he wanted to find Shan Dara, it was more important they leave for the meeting, now. He trotted back to the mesquite. "We need to get going," he said to the young cats, then reluctantly looked at the bird. "This is probably where we part company."

In a neighboring oak the possum stretched on a sturdy branch, crunching the last remains of the snake. "You're leaving?" he called.

Buddy felt a stab of sadness. "Yes. Where we're going won't be safe for you."

Jaws still working, the possum chewed thoughtfully.

"There's one thing, though," Buddy said. "I know you're both ready to get home, but would you mind waiting for us in the pecan grove? If we don't show up by dawn"—he let out a slow, even breath—"you and the bird should go. But if we do return, there's one last thing I'd like to ask of you."

"Sure," the possum said, clamoring to the ground and joining them. "Just name it."

"Would you make sure that Zekki and Pris get back to Sixth Avenue? It's not too far from here." Buddy stopped, suddenly choked with emotion. "And—and I'd appreciate knowing that they're back with The Boy and okay."

The bird and possum looked at one another, then nodded solemnly.

Buddy felt a wave of relief. "Thanks. Thanks for everything you've done. Both of you."

The possum's friendly face wrinkled in a smile. "You'll be fine. Like my mother always said: 'No matter how much you wish they wouldn't, cats always come back.'" He belched happily. "No offense."

The mockingbird flapped to the ground, eyes riveted on Buddy. "I'd like to come, but if you don't think I should . . . then I won't." She puffed her feathers. "We'll be waiting by the fence where we all crossed the highway. Good luck."

"But we're all going home together, right?" Pris asked.

Buddy rubbed his head against her shoulder. "We'll talk about that later."

"I don't understand," Zekki said. "Where are we going?"

"You've always wanted to see The Cat Master. Well, tonight is the night."

Zekki frowned. "But you said no one could find Him."

"You can't." Buddy smiled and stared at the moon. "But once in a while . . . He finds you."

The rat had definitely seen him. It rose on scrawny haunches, nose twitching, long brown tail snaking in the dust. There was nowhere to run, and Orie had a fleeting thought of Tenba and the incredible bravery she had shown. If this was the end, so be it. At least he would go in a way she could be proud of. Taking a deep breath, he moved from the weeds and stepped boldly into the open.

The rat pulled its lips over pointed teeth and shrank back.

"Come over here, you laboratory reject!" Orie shouted. "You want some action?" He turned his back, wiggling his tail stump in an obscene bump and grind. "Action this!"

The moon drifted behind a cloud, and the alley dropped into darkness.

Lowering itself onto all fours, the rat squinted for a better look, then licked its lips and smirked. "I'm gonna enjoy this."

"That's funny," a voice sounded from behind a clump of weeds. "I was just thinking the same thing." A small brown body bolted from the darkness, snapped the rodent's neck with one neat jerk, and tossed it on the ground. It twitched and kicked, mouth still cracked in an evil grin.

"Frank!" Orie cried, running into the alley and leaping with joy at the Dachshund's sturdy feet. "What are you doing here?"

"Oh, cruising around." Furrowing his brow, the dog

looked surprised. "You mean you haven't seen the posters?"

Orie blinked in bewilderment

"The lost-dog posters. They're all over the place." He lowered his head, silky ears touching the ground. "Seriously, you haven't seen them? Full-color photo, lots of pleading. There's a reward and everything." His eyes became hooded and sly. "So, where's my big ol' Fräulein?" Prancing along the chain-link, he snuffled in the shadows. "Come out, come out, Uncle Frank's got something for you." He stopped and trotted back to the lizard. "Where is she?"

"She isn't here. She's—she got hurt."

The little dog stepped back, lips raised in a snarl. "Who hurt her? I'll rip 'em to shreds!"

"You don't have to." Orie puffed with pride. "She already did. She killed the chow. I thought she had died, too, but Animal Control came the next morning and said she was alive." His voice quivered. "Then they took her away."

"Whoa, killed the chow." Frank whistled in awe. "What a babe!"

"The thing is," Orie said, "I've been trying to get home since this morning to see her." He gave a nod in the dead rat's direction. "But things have gotten a little unpredictable here, if you know what I mean, and I'm not making very good time."

"No problem." The Dachshund gave an amiable shake. "I'll give you a ride." He shrugged, lifting his hind leg over the dandelion. "I was going home tomorrow anyway."

Orie clambered onto his back, and after one last sniff at the rat, they turned and headed up the alley.

"She'll be okay, lizard," Frank boomed, bounding

through a backyard and galloping down a driveway. "Those German girls are built to last!"

Buddy led the way up the embankment, zigzagging over rocks and weeds and waiting patiently as Zekki and Pris scrambled behind. "Follow me until I tell you to stop. When I do, don't go any farther. Do you understand?"

The young cats nodded dumbly, then fell into line, ears nervously flicking back and forth.

It didn't take long to backtrack across the golf course, only this time, instead of veering off the path, which would have led to the pecan grove, they continued walking. From somewhere in the distance, faint rumblings drifted in the air.

Zekki and Pris stopped and crouched to the ground.

"What is that?" the calico whispered.

Zekki cocked his ears. "I don't know, but it seems sort of familiar."

They trotted across freshly cut grass, the summer night fragrant with the smells of water and jasmine. Abruptly the greens gave way to sand, and the three animals stopped at the base of a sloping hill they had seen from the orchard. Instead of climbing to the top, Buddy walked around it, coming to a halt on the other side.

The young cats tumbled after him, then stopped, gasping at what they saw.

Clustered around the base of the hill and trailing into the distance were hundreds of cats.

"There're so many," Zekki said with wonder. He turned in each direction, seeing cats of every description, age, and breed.

Felines clustered by the banks of a pond, crouched by thickets lining the fairways, and skulked through the lush landscape separating houses from greens. Their purring escalated, rising from the golf course like velvet smoke, drifting over the trees and beyond.

Buddy turned and nudged Zekki's shoulder. "If I don't come back, can you find your way to the possum and mockingbird?"

Zekki nodded, his breathing ragged with stress. "Yes, but—"

"Good," Buddy interrupted gently, touching his nose to each of theirs. "Stay here."

Stunned, the two young cats watched as Buddy made his way through the soft mass of bodies that first blocked, then yielded to him, as he disappeared into the crowd.

Pris was jostled to her right, then pushed to her knees by a new wave of cats streaming toward the hill from every direction. "What's happening?" she called to Zekki who also fought to keep his balance against the crush of bodies.

"Quiet!" an ancient Burmese hissed. "We're here to see The Cat Master; have some respect."

"But where is he?" Pris whispered.

"There." The Burmese moved to the side so they could have a better view of the figure that strode firmly to the top of the hill.

Pris stared in wonder. "But that's Buddy!"

"Yes," said the cat. "He's come home."

THIRTY-FOUR

BUDDY WAITED ON THE MOUND, silently observing the scene below.

Cats of all descriptions covered the golf course, eyes gleaming in the moonlight, coats illuminated in its silver glow. Furiously kneading the grass, they clawed the fairways until dirt flew in all directions and the humid air vibrated with rumbling purrs from a thousand throats.

A powerful figure pushed through the crowd and leaped close to where Buddy stood on the knoll.

The purring stopped, replaced by a watchful quiet.

Savoring the moment, Jett took a long look at the expectant faces surrounding him. All the planning, pain, and injustice had been worth it. Tonight his reign would begin. He tossed his head in triumph. "You know me!" he bellowed to the crowd.

"Yes," came the breathy response.

"I have walked among you, I have been faithful." Ears

flattened, he turned toward Buddy. "But not him."

Voices murmured from below.

"This imposter!" Jett spat, face twisted with rage. "This imposter appears after two long years hoping you won't ask where he's been! And why?" Jett's empty socket was hollow in the moonlight. "Because he abandoned you for a human and the mindless life of the Indoor!" The tom paced in the grass, eye locked on the cats below. "Ask him. Ask the deserter where he's been and what he did in the time he was away."

Hundreds of bodies strained toward Buddy for an answer, tails twitching, whiskers fanned and alert.

The yellow tom moved forward. "It's true I lived with humans, and it's true I questioned my past as well as my future." He looked steadily at the crowd. "But there is no shame in not knowing, the shame lies in not seeking. I have heard The Cat Master's voice, as you all have. He has spoken to me of my destiny, and I stand before you, ready to serve."

"Well, lucky us!" Jett roared from the shadows. "So now he's ready! What about tomorrow and the next day and the next? When will this pretender tire of his 'future,' as he puts it, and abandon you again for the life he truly craves? He doesn't have the stomach for the Outs!" Jett spewed, spittle webbing on his whiskers in glistening drops. "He's nothing but a mewling, lap-sitting Indoor!"

"Death to the Indoors!" someone shouted from the crowd.

"Feral thug!" came a shrieking reply.

Jett paced in long, muscular strides along the precipice. "They are the fat, the weak, and the stupid, begging for scraps from the table of our enemy, and he is one of them—"

"Don't be manipulated by the poison of prejudice!" Buddy interrupted. "Indoors are also our brothers, and there are many here tonight who live both lives. Be honest, what Feral has never longed for the warmth of a fireplace in the dead of winter, or water and shade in the heat of summer?"

Glowing eyes blinked, and the night rumbled with mutterings of agreement.

"The Indoors' ways are different," Buddy continued, "but feline is feline, and the children of The Wind follow many paths. It's true that I've lived as an Indoor, but I was born a Feral. I believe the old Master chose me for this very reason. The respect I have for both worlds will bring us closer, with an understanding that will serve us all." He paused. "There is no need for fighting between us."

A few cats in the front row nodded.

"Don't—don't believe his lies!" Jett stammered. "Any information he has will serve him, not you! Remember The Law! Only a Feral can be Cat Master! Is this imposter a Feral? Look at him! Smell him! The stench of the Indoors follows him like a dog!" He scanned the greens, eye narrowed with cunning. "Let his past be your warning, my friends. He abandoned his mate in the alley, and he'll abandon you!"

"Ahn-ya!" voices repeated from the fairway.

"Yes, Ahn-ya, dead and forgotten, and now he has chosen another . . . an *Indoor*." He glared into the darkness. "Is this not proof of his true allegiance? Ferals do not mix with *Indoors*, this is The Law!" Stalking back and forth, his eye gleamed red and unearthly. "Ferals do not mix with *humans*, this is The Law!"

Hundreds of voices meowed in agreement.

"To survive is also The Law!" Buddy cried. "My allegiance is toward all felines, and I make no distinction between Feral and Indoor." He pushed past Jett, his eyes locked on the throng below. "It is the Feral way to walk alone, but by choice, not edict. Indoors live with a burden of constraint we can't imagine, and their lives offer lessons in acceptance without servitude. Never forget there are humans capable of love and respect." He looked pointedly at Jett. "Just as there are cats who are treacherous and cruel."

The crowd shifted uncomfortably.

"I was near death," Buddy continued, voice hoarse with emotion. "And a human found me, nursed me to health, and protected me. This is the reason I had to leave Ahn-ya, and this is the reason I left you. I proudly love The Boy who saved me. He is gentle, honest, and protective of all living things." Raising his head with defiance, he turned to Jett. "As for the Indoor Shan Dara: She has chosen the feral way of her own free will. This is in accordance with The Law. Now she is in danger, put there by the very one who seeks to lead you, and I demand her freedom!" Lashing his tail, Buddy crouched low. "Where is she, Jett?"

The big tom shrugged. "Perhaps she's where all who've

trusted you have ended." His eye glittered with malice. "With Ahn-ya, dead in the alley."

"That's not true!" a voice shouted from below.

Swiveling toward the sound, Jett's face was blank and suddenly uncertain.

An emaciated figure limped through the crowd, a pale shape moving behind him. "The Siamese isn't dead! I've been hiding her in the orchard!"

"Soot!" Zekki called, as Shan Dara burst past the black cat and leaped up the hill to Buddy's side.

Fur bristled, Jett hissed with fury. "Traitor! You've shamed the memory of Ahn-ya, for the one who betrayed her!"

"No!" Soot pulled himself to the knoll with effort. "To harm my own kind would have shamed my mother." He turned toward The Gathering. "My mother always told me about a yellow tom whom she'd loved since kittenhood; a cat that Jett hated, ambushed, and left in a dumpster to die. I didn't realize she was talking about Buddy until now."

"You can't believe this pathetic sycophant! It was Buddy who attacked *me*!" Jett pushed forward, desperately scanning the crowd with his weeping socket. "See my face? He did it! Blinded his own brother because Ahn-ya loved me more!"

"That's a lie!" Soot put full weight on his injured leg, bracing for an assault. "It was you who attacked Buddy. Ahn-ya followed you both to the golf course that day. She saw the whole thing." He dipped his head, voice low. "I know you're my father, Jett, but I can't lie."

"He's not your father," Buddy said. "I am."

Soot stared, mouth agape.

"Don't listen to him!" Jett shouted. "I'm your flesh and blood; your loyalty is to me!"

"You—you mean" the black cat stammered "I—I'm not . . . ?"

"No." Shan Dara moved from the shadows. "Buddy's telling you the truth. You really are his son; you don't owe Jett anything!"

"Shut up, you stupid Indoor!" Jett turned on the Siamese and sprang forward. "I should have killed you myself!"

"Move!" Buddy pushed Shan Dara out of the way, meeting Jett's assault in midair.

The night reverberated with the sound of their impact, and a blast of wind swept through the golf course.

The onlookers squinted through the dust, straining to see as Jett and Buddy tumbled down the hill. Their growls and screams blended with yowls of surprise, as the crowd parted, watching the brothers roll onto the greens, their teeth bared, their tails lashing with fury.

Buddy grabbed Jett's neck, but the big cat twirled in his grasp, breaking loose and running from the knoll.

"They're headed toward the pond!" a voice cried from the crowd.

The two cats zigzagged through foliage and vaulted onto an oak tree by the water. Furiously they climbed, their paws slipping on bark as twigs caught in their coats. With a burst of speed, Jett shimmied ahead, blocking Buddy from climbing higher and forcing him onto a decaying branch that hung over the pond.

Jett looked down at the crowd now assembled below. "Everyone's watching, Brother." His eye glowed with satisfaction. "Let's show them who the real Cat Master is." With a grunt he lunged toward Buddy, his jaws open, ready to strike.

A gust of wind shook the tree, and Jett landed short, desperately struggling for a foothold. The branches whipped and lashed beneath Mother's power, until suddenly, the limb snapped in half, spilling both cats into the pond below.

Water gushed up Buddy's nose and down his throat as he thrashed to the surface, but Jett's powerful claws snagged his neck, dragging him down. Colors flashed behind Buddy's eyes, and he realized he was losing consciousness. *No!* his mind shouted. *Of all his blood, you were chosen!* Twisting forward Buddy sank his fangs into the big cat's shoulder, and with every ounce of energy left, pushed his brother under. Blood filled his mouth as Jett bucked and rolled, trying to escape, but Buddy held fast, his own lungs about to burst, until finally the struggling subsided, and Jett floated limply beneath him, his body still at last.

Buddy pushed upward, mouth gasping for air, paws slapping the water's surface in fast, desperate strokes. With one final kick his toes touched mud and pebbles, and he collapsed in the shallows, heaving for air.

The Wind slowed to a gentle breeze, and Buddy staggered to his feet. Behind him the moon peeked between tattered clouds, its beams reflecting off the pond. Jett's body bobbed in the water, his paws undulating with the current, his eyeless socket turned toward the sky.

One by one, the cats of The Gathering encircled the pond. Eyes huge with wonder, they stared first at Jett's lifeless form, then at the silent figure poised on the bank.

Shan Dara moved toward Buddy and turned to the crowd. "The Master has spoken and The Gathering must answer." Sinking to her haunches, she bowed her head. "Hail The Cat Master!"

The Master, The Master! chanted the cats, their thoughts rising through the air, crossing oceans and continents, circling the globe.

We are legion! Mind-talk soared from barnyards and alleys. *Now we are one!*

"One! One!" sang the humming reply.

Buddy watched the swaying mass of bodies and felt his exhaustion replaced by a raw and tingling strength. Water streamed from his coat as he strode to the top of the knoll and turned to the throng beneath him. "I bring you the promise of The Cat Master!" he roared.

"The Master," voices purred from the fairways.

"As long as I live, you will never walk alone!"

In laboratories and shelters, cats crouched in the dark. "We are never alone," they chanted.

"Live your lives with honor and endure your pain with courage!" Buddy's eyes burned fierce and bright. "For your voice is my voice, and our minds are one!"

"Pain with courage," a dying stray whispered.

"His voice is ours," Zekki and Pris intoned, surprised to know words they had never been taught but were destined to say all their lives.

Soot, who had been watching from the shadows, quietly turned from the crowd and headed toward the orchard.

"Hail, Soot!" Buddy said loudly.

The black cat looked back in astonishment.

Shan Dara lifted her paw. "Hail, Soot! Heir to the Master, son of Ahn-ya!"

"Prince of the Alleys!" the cats chanted as Soot's eyes met Buddy's. "He stands with the Master!"

Soot waited, acknowledging the cheers, then with green eyes glowing in the moonlight, he limped proudly up the hill to his father's side.

"Hail The Cat Master!" he shouted, head high, tail erect. "He walks among us at last!"

THIRTY-FIVE

THE NIGHT'S EVENTS FELT surreal to Zekki. Buddy's ascension to Cat Master had been followed by a wild celebration. Thousands of cats gathered on fairways, rolling with ecstasy in the grass and dragging prey from the bushes. Throughout the festivities, Buddy and Shan Dara remained separate from the revelry, watching quietly from the knoll and only occasionally speaking with the cats that Soot escorted to them.

No one went near the pond.

Just as sunrise glistened behind gauzy clouds and the last cat disappeared into the shadows, Zekki and Pris staggered to the orchard, where the mockingbird and possum were waiting.

Buddy was The Cat Master.

Jett was dead.

The whole thing was so unbelievable that if Pris hadn't confirmed what Zekki had seen, the white tom might have written the whole thing off as hallucination. Even so, both knew what they had witnessed had changed them forever, and in a strange and poignant way, it had changed Buddy, too. Though Buddy, Shan Dara, and Soot followed the

young cats back to the orchard, there had been little conversation among them. The trio had secluded themselves
beneath a stand of ferns, where they now lay talking, their
voices barely a hum above the rustling of leaves. Zekki
longed to join them, but an unquestioned distance stood
between them, one he instinctively knew could never be
breached.

The possum lurched to his feet. "I need to get going."
He glanced at the bird, who nodded in agreement. "We've
talked to Buddy, and we'll be glad to take you back across the
highway, if that's what you want."

Pris took a hesitant step, then stopped. "Is it?" she said,
turning to Zekki. "Is that what we want?"

He took a deep breath. How long had it been since he'd
stared through windows, his eyes fixed on the alleys, his ears
tuned to the mysterious sounds beckoning from the distance? How long had he ached to be among the wild things
scurrying in the darkness, his days filled with danger and
adventure?

"Well?" The mockingbird fluttered to the ground.

Pris's questioning eyes bore into Zekki's, and his brain
scrambled for answers. *What do I want?* he thought. *What
do I do?*

You've dreamed of freedom, a familiar voice buzzed in his
head. *Now you have it.*

Zekki started, his heart pumping with fear. What had he
just heard?

Mind-talk, the voice answered gently. *We're speaking with
our minds.*

The white cat turned to Pris, waiting for her to acknowl-
edge what had just happened; then realized it wasn't possible

for her to know. Buddy was speaking to him in the language of telepathy, something the white cat had witnessed as part of The Gathering, but never in private conversation. Zekki's blue eyes squeezed shut, as he concentrated in earnest. *What—what if I was wrong about freedom? Maybe I don't want it anymore.*

But it's already yours. Buddy's words had a soothing, hypnotic quality that rose and fell with the sweet-smelling breeze blowing through the orchard.

Blinking against the urge to sleep, Zekki finally surrendered, enjoying the enveloping warmth of the sun on his ears and nose. His thoughts trailed in dreamy wisps behind half-closed eyes. *I don't understand,* he thought.

Freedom isn't what you choose. Buddy's voice blended with the wind, its cool breeze wafting against his cheek. *Freedom is having the choice.*

The words echoed in his mind, and Zekki shook himself. The stand of ferns where he had seen Buddy, Shan Dara, and Soot was now empty. Something shone against the grass, and the white cat moved closer. It was Shan Dara's golden collar; the last remaining link to her former life. Zekki looked toward the highway. And what of his and Pris's former lives? He thought of home and The Boy.

Summer was over and soon fall would come, bringing sweaters and school and books tumbling from backpacks. Winter would follow, wrapping the house in the smoky scents of burning wood and cinnamon, and just when it seemed nothing could ever grow again, the old magnolia would burst with creamy flowers and geraniums would appear on the porch, their ruffled blooms laced with butter-flies. Pris and Zekki had promised to take care of The Boy if Buddy didn't return, and suddenly Zekki's heart ached with longing for the little house and the loving humans who lived there.

"We have to leave," the mockingbird called. "Are you coming?" She cocked her head. "Or are you staying?"

Zekki looked into Pris's trusting face and smiled. "We're going home," he said, touching his nose to hers. "We're going home."

EPILOGUE

THE SEASONS CAME AND WENT on Sixth Avenue. From their places by the window, Pris and Zekki watched the years roll by.

The Boy left home, the magnolia died and was replaced by a sycamore, and Buddy's photo on the wall faded beneath a sprinkle of dust in the hallway.

On autumn nights when the moon glowed round and golden in crisp October skies, dark memories of another orb would invade their dreams, and the two cats would jolt from sleep, expecting Jett to spring from the shadows.

Tenba lived one more summer, and after her passing, Orie disappeared. As far as the cats knew, no other lizard ever inhabited the crawl space, though each summer many of his kind gathered in the yard to pay homage to "He Who Was Special," and the cats would cuddle in the darkness, listening to long-winded stories of the Legendary Lizard and how he had ridden to battle on the great warrior dog to save the Kingdom of the Felines.

Now and then, a wandering Feral would stop and share

the latest gossip. A yellow tom and a Siamese had been spotted in China, The Crippled Prince now ruled the alleys since the old woman's death, and it was rumored that Animal Control had trapped the possum, though no one knew for sure. Frank continued his escapades well into middle age, and for a time, the cats saw the mockingbird in her mournful wanderings, but she never stopped, and they understood.

Occasionally, when the evenings were hot and still, a sudden wind would gust through the holly, and they would stare out the window, wondering if they were dreaming or if they'd really seen a blur of yellow beneath the hedge.

It was at these times they remembered The Promise made that summer long ago, when three cats, two dogs, a possum, bird, and lizard restored a monarch to his rightful throne . . . and it was this memory that kept their old hearts beating and their eyes turned with hope toward Sho-valla.

Zekki

Mockingbirds

Frank

Possum

Chow
mix